14 S0-BJM-968

DISCARDED

FICTION

Dradin, in Love

The Book of Lost Places (stories)

Veniss Underground

City of Saints and Madmen

Secret Life (stories)

Shriek: An Afterword

The Situation

Finch

The Third Bear (stories)

NONFICTION

Why Should I Cut Your Throat?

Booklife: Strategies and Survival Tips for the 21st-Century Writer

Monstrous Creatures

The Steampunk Bible: An Illustrated Guide to the World of Imaginary Airships, Corsets and Goggles, Mad Scientists, and Strange Literature

Wonderbook: The Illustrated Guide to Creating Imaginative Fiction

ANNIHILATION

ANNIH

ILATION

JEFF VANDERMEER

HarperCollins*Publishers*Ltd

Published by HarperCollins Publishers Ltd by arrangement
with Farrar, Straus and Giroux, LLC.

First Canadian edition

HarperCollins books may be purchased for educational, business or
sales promotional use through our Special Markets Department.

HarperCollins Publishers Ltd
2 Bloor Street East, 20th Floor
Toronto, Ontario, Canada
M4W 1A8

www.harpercollins.ca

Library and Archives Canada Cataloguing in Publication
information is available upon request

ISBN 978-1-44342-839-2

Designed by Abby Kagan

Printed and bound in Canada
WC 9 8 7 6 5 4 3 2 1

For Ann

ANNIHILATION

01: INITIATION

The tower, which was not supposed to be there, plunges into the earth in a place just before the black pine forest begins to give way to swamp and then the reeds and wind-gnarled trees of the marsh flats. Beyond the marsh flats and the natural canals lies the ocean and, a little farther down the coast, a derelict lighthouse. All of this part of the country had been abandoned for decades, for reasons that are not easy to relate. Our expedition was the first to enter Area X for more than two years, and much of our predecessors' equipment had rusted, their tents and sheds little more than husks. Looking out over that untroubled landscape, I do not believe any of us could yet see the threat.

There were four of us: a biologist, an anthropologist, a surveyor, and a psychologist. I was the biologist. All of us were women this time, chosen as part of the complex set of variables that governed sending the expeditions. The psychologist, who was older than the rest of us, served as the expedition's leader. She had put us all under hypnosis to cross the border, to make sure we remained calm. It took four days of hard hiking after crossing the border to reach the coast.

Our mission was simple: to continue the government's investigation into the mysteries of Area X, slowly working our way out from base camp.

The expedition could last days, months, or even years, depending on various stimuli and conditions. We had supplies with us for six months, and another two years' worth of supplies had already been stored at the base camp. We had also been assured that it was safe to live off the land if necessary. All of our foodstuffs were smoked or canned or in packets. Our most outlandish equipment consisted of a measuring device that had been issued to each of us, which hung from a strap on our belts: a small rectangle of black metal with a glass-covered hole in the middle. If the hole glowed red, we had thirty minutes to remove ourselves to "a safe place." We were not told what the device measured or why we should be afraid should it glow red. After the first few hours, I had grown so used to it that I hadn't looked at it again. We had been forbidden watches and compasses.

When we reached the camp, we set about replacing obsolete or damaged equipment with what we had brought and putting up our own tents. We would rebuild the sheds later, once we were sure that Area X had not affected us. The members of the last expedition had eventually drifted off, one by one. Over time, they had returned to their families, so strictly speaking they did not vanish. They simply disappeared from Area X and, by unknown means, reappeared back in the world beyond the border. They could not relate the specifics of that journey. This *transference* had taken place across a period of eighteen months, and it was not something that had been experienced by prior expeditions. But other phenomena could also result in "premature dissolution of expeditions," as our superiors put it, so we needed to test our stamina for that place.

We also needed to acclimate ourselves to the environment. In the forest near base camp one might encounter black bears or coyotes. You might hear a sudden croak and watch a night heron startle from a tree branch and, distracted, step on a poisonous snake, of which there were at least six varieties. Bogs and streams hid huge aquatic reptiles, and so we were careful not to wade too deep to collect our water samples. Still, these aspects of the ecosystem did not really concern any of us. Other elements had the ability to unsettle, however. Long ago, towns had existed here, and we encountered eerie signs of human habitation: rotting cabins with sunken, red-tinged roofs, rusted wagon-wheel spokes half-buried in the dirt, and the barely seen outlines of what used to be enclosures for livestock, now mere ornament for layers of pine-needle loam.

Far worse, though, was a low, powerful moaning at dusk. The wind off the sea and the odd interior stillness dulled our ability to gauge direction, so that the sound seemed to infiltrate the black water that soaked the cypress trees. This water was so dark we could see our faces in it, and it never stirred, set like glass, reflecting the beards of gray moss that smothered the cypress trees. If you looked out through these areas, toward the ocean, all you saw was the black water, the gray of the cypress trunks, and the constant, motionless rain of moss flowing down. All you heard was the low moaning.

The effect of this cannot be understood without being there. The beauty of it cannot be understood, either, and when you see beauty in desolation it changes something inside you. Desolation tries to colonize you.

As noted, we found the tower in a place just before the forest became waterlogged and then turned to salt marsh. This occurred on our fourth day after reaching base camp, by which time we had almost gotten our bearings. We did not expect to find anything there, based on both the maps that we brought with us and the water-stained, pine-dust-smeared documents our predecessors had left behind. But there it was, surrounded by a fringe of scrub grass, half-hidden by fallen moss off to the left of the trail: a circular block of some grayish stone seeming to mix cement and ground-up seashells. It measured roughly sixty feet in diameter, this circular block, and was raised from ground level by about eight inches. Nothing had been etched into or written on its surface that could in any way reveal its purpose or the identity of its makers. Starting at due north, a rectangular opening set into the surface of the block revealed stairs spiraling down into darkness. The entrance was obscured by the webs of banana spiders and debris from storms, but a cool draft came from below.

At first, only I saw it as a tower. I don't know why the word *tower* came to me, given that it tunneled into the ground. I could as easily have considered it a bunker or a submerged building. Yet as soon as I saw the staircase, I remembered the lighthouse on the coast and had a sudden vision of the last expedition drifting off, one by one, and sometime thereafter the ground shifting in a uniform and preplanned way to leave the lighthouse standing where it had always been but depositing this underground part of it inland. I saw this in vast and intricate detail as we all stood there, and, looking back, I mark it as the first irrational thought I had once we had reached our destination.

"This is impossible," said the surveyor, staring at her maps. The solid shade of late afternoon cast her in cool darkness and lent the words more urgency than they would have had otherwise. The sun was telling us that soon we'd have to use our flashlights to interrogate the impossible, although I'd have been perfectly happy doing it in the dark.

"And yet there it is," I said. "Unless we are having a mass hallucination."

"The architectural model is hard to identify," the anthropologist said. "The materials are ambiguous, indicating local origin but not necessarily local construction. Without going inside, we will not know if it is primitive or modern, or something in between. I'm not sure I would want to guess at how old it is, either."

We had no way to inform our superiors about this discovery. One rule for an expedition into Area X was that we were to attempt no outside contact, for fear of some irrevocable contamination. We also took little with us that matched our current level of technology. We had no cell or satellite phones, no computers, no camcorders, no complex measuring instruments except for those strange black boxes hanging from our belts. Our cameras required a makeshift darkroom. The absence of cell phones in particular made the real world seem very far away to the others, but I had always preferred to live without them. For weapons, we had knives, a locked container of antique handguns, and one assault rifle, this last a reluctant concession to current security standards.

It was expected simply that we would keep a record, like this one, in a journal, like this one: lightweight but nearly indestructible, with waterproof paper, a flexible black-and-white cover, and the blue horizontal lines for writing and the red line to the left to mark the margin. These journals would either return with us or be recovered by the next expedition. We had been cautioned to provide maximum context, so that anyone ignorant of Area X could understand our accounts. We had also been ordered not to share our journal entries with one another. Too much shared information could skew our observations, our superiors believed. But I knew from experience how hopeless this pursuit, this attempt to weed out bias, was. Nothing that lived and breathed was truly objective—even in a vacuum, even if all that possessed the brain was a self-immolating desire for the truth.

"I'm excited by this discovery," the psychologist interjected before we had discussed the tower much further. "Are you excited, too?" She had not asked us that particular question before. During training, she had tended to ask questions more like "How calm do you think you might be in an emergency?" Back then, I had felt as if she were a bad actor, playing a role. Now it seemed even more apparent, as if being our leader somehow made her nervous.

"It is definitely exciting . . . and unexpected," I said, trying not to mock her and failing, a little. I was surprised to feel a sense of growing unease, mostly because in my imagination, my dreams, this discovery would have been among the more banal. In my head, before we had crossed the border, I had seen so many things: vast cities, peculiar animals, and, once, during a period of illness, an enormous monster that rose from the waves to bear down on our camp.

The surveyor, meanwhile, just shrugged and would not answer the psychologist's question. The anthropologist nodded as if she agreed with me. The entrance to the tower leading down exerted a kind of presence, a blank surface that let us write so many things upon it. This presence manifested like a low-grade fever, pressing down on all of us.

I would tell you the names of the other three, if it mattered, but only the surveyor would last more than the next day or two. Besides, we were always strongly discouraged from using names: We were meant to be focused on our purpose, and "anything personal should be left behind." Names belonged to where we had come from, not to who we were while embedded in Area X.

Originally our expedition had numbered five and included a linguist. To reach the border, we each had to enter a separate bright white room with a door at the far end and a single metal chair in the corner. The chair had holes along the sides for straps; the implications of this raised a prickle of alarm, but by then I was set in my determination to reach Area X. The facility that housed these rooms was under the control of the Southern Reach, the clandestine government agency that dealt with all matters connected to Area X.

There we waited while innumerable readings were taken and various blasts of air, some cool, some hot, pressed down on us from vents in the ceiling. At some point, the psychologist visited each of us, although I do not remember what was said. Then we exited through the far door into a central staging area, with double doors at the end of a long hallway.

The psychologist greeted us there, but the linguist never reappeared.

"She had second thoughts," the psychologist told us, meeting our questions with a firm gaze. "She decided to stay behind." This came as a small shock, but there was also relief that it had not been someone else. Of all of our skill sets, linguist seemed at the time most expendable.

After a moment, the psychologist said, "Now, clear your minds." This meant she would begin the process of hypnotizing us so we could cross the border. She would then put herself under a kind of self-hypnosis. It had been explained that we would need to cross the border with precautions to protect against our minds tricking us. Apparently hallucinations were common. At least, this was what they told us. I no longer can be sure it was the truth. The actual nature of the border had been withheld from us for security reasons; we knew only that it was invisible to the naked eye.

So when I "woke up" with the others, it was in full gear, including heavy hiking boots, with the weight of forty-pound backpacks and a multitude of additional supplies hanging from our belts. All three of us lurched, and the anthropologist fell to one knee, while the psychologist patiently waited for us to recover. "I'm sorry," she said. "That was the least startling reentry I could manage."

The surveyor cursed, and glared at her. She had a temper that must have been deemed an asset. The anthropologist, as was her way, got to her feet, uncomplaining. And I, as was my way, was too busy observing to take this rude awakening personally. For example, I noticed the cruelty of the almost imperceptible smile on the psychologist's lips as she watched us struggle to adjust, the anthropologist still floundering and apologizing for floundering. Later I realized I might have misread her expression; it might have been pained or self-pitying.

We were on a dirt trail strewn with pebbles, dead leaves, and pine needles damp to the touch. Velvet ants and tiny emerald beetles crawled over them. The tall pines, with their scaly ridges of bark, rose on both sides, and the shadows of flying birds conjured lines between them. The air was so fresh it buffeted the lungs and we strained to breathe for a few seconds, mostly from surprise. Then, after marking our location with a piece of red cloth tied to a tree, we began to walk forward, into the unknown. If the psychologist somehow became incapacitated and could not lead us across at the end of our mission, we had been told to return to await "extraction." No one ever explained what form "extraction" might take, but the implication was that our superiors could observe the extraction point from afar, even though it was inside the border.

We had been told not to look back upon arrival, but I snuck a glance anyway, while the psychologist's attention was elsewhere. I don't know quite what I saw. It was hazy, indistinct, and already far behind us—perhaps a gate, perhaps a trick of the eye. Just a sudden impression of a fizzing block of light, fast fading.

The reasons I had volunteered were very separate from my qualifications for the expedition. I believe I qualified because I specialized in transitional environments, and this particular location transitioned several times, meaning that it was home to a complexity of ecosystems. In few other places could you still find habitat where, within the space of walking only six or seven miles, you went from forest to swamp to salt marsh to beach. In Area X, I had been told, I would find marine life that had adjusted to the brackish freshwater and which at low tide swam far up the natural canals formed by the reeds, sharing the same environment with otters and deer. If you walked along the beach, riddled through with the holes of fiddler crabs, you would sometimes look out to see one of the giant reptiles, for they, too, had adapted to their habitat.

I understood why no one lived in Area X now, that it was pristine because of that reason, but I kept un-remembering it. I had decided instead to make believe that it was simply a protected wildlife refuge, and we were hikers who happened to be scientists. This made sense on another level: We did not know what had happened here, what was still happening here, and any preformed theories would affect my analysis of the evidence as we encountered it. Besides, for my part it hardly mattered what lies I told myself because my existence back in the world had become at least as empty as Area X. With nothing left to anchor me, I *needed* to be here. As for the others, I don't know what they told themselves, and I didn't want to know, but I believe they all at least pretended to some level of curiosity. Curiosity could be a powerful distraction.

That night we talked about the tower, although the other three insisted on calling it a tunnel. The responsibility for the thrust of our investigations resided with each individual, the psychologist's authority describing a wider circle around these decisions. Part of the current rationale for sending the expeditions lay in giving each member some autonomy to decide, which helped to increase "the possibility of significant variation."

This vague protocol existed in the context of our separate skill sets. For example, although we had all received basic weapons and survival training, the surveyor had far more medical and firearms experience than the rest of us. The anthropologist had once been an architect; indeed, she had years ago survived a fire in a building she had designed, the only really personal thing I had found out about her. As for the psychologist, we knew the least about her, but I think we all believed she came from some kind of management background.

The discussion of the tower was, in a way, our first opportunity to test the limits of disagreement and of compromise.

"I don't think we should focus on the tunnel," the anthropologist said. "We should explore farther first, and we should come back to it with whatever data we gather from our other investigations—including of the lighthouse."

How predictable, and yet perhaps prescient, for the anthropologist to try to substitute a safer, more comfortable option. Although the idea of mapping seemed perfunctory or repetitive to me, I could not deny the existence of the tower, of which there was no suggestion on any map.

Then the surveyor spoke. "In this case I feel that we should rule out the tunnel as something invasive or threatening. Before we explore farther. It's like an enemy at our backs otherwise, if we press forward." She had come to us from the military, and I could see already the value of that experience. I had thought a surveyor would always side with the idea of further exploration, so this opinion carried weight.

"I'm impatient to explore the habitats here," I said. "But in a sense, given that it is not noted on any map, the 'tunnel' . . . or tower . . . seems important. It is either a deliberate exclusion from our maps and thus known . . . and that is a message of sorts . . . or it is something new that wasn't here when the last expedition arrived."

The surveyor gave me a look of thanks for the support, but my position had nothing to do with helping her. Something about the idea of a tower that headed straight down played with a twinned sensation of vertigo and a fascination with structure. I could not tell which part I craved and which I feared, and I kept seeing the inside of nautilus shells and other naturally occurring patterns balanced against a sudden leap off a cliff into the unknown.

The psychologist nodded, appeared to consider these opinions, and asked, "Does anyone yet have even an inkling of a sensation of wanting to leave?" It was a legitimate question, but jarring nonetheless.

All three of us shook our heads.

"What about you?" the surveyor asked the psychologist. "What is your opinion?"

The psychologist grinned, which seemed odd. But she must have known any one of us might have been tasked with observing her own reactions to stimuli. Perhaps the idea that a surveyor, an expert in the surface of things, might have been chosen, rather than a biologist or anthropologist, amused her. "I must admit to feeling a great deal of unease at the moment. But I am unsure whether it is because of the effect of the overall environment or the presence of the tunnel. Personally, I would like to rule out the tunnel."

Tower.

"Three to one, then," the anthropologist said, clearly relieved that the decision had been made for her.

The surveyor just shrugged.

Perhaps I'd been wrong about curiosity. The surveyor didn't seem curious about anything.

"Bored?" I asked.

"Eager to get on with it," she said, to the group, as if I'd asked the question for all of us.

We were in the communal tent for our talk. It had become dark by then and there came soon after the strange mournful call in the night that we knew must have natural causes but created a little shiver regardless. As if that was the signal to disband, we went back to our own quarters to be alone with our thoughts. I lay awake in my tent for a while trying to turn the tower into a tunnel, or even a shaft, but with no success. Instead, my mind kept returning to a question: *What lies hidden at its base?*

During our hike from the border to the base camp near the coast, we had experienced almost nothing out of the ordinary. The birds sang as they should; the deer took flight, their white tails exclamation points against the green and brown of the underbrush; the raccoons, bowlegged, swayed about their business, ignoring us. As a group, we felt almost giddy, I think, to be free after so many confining months of training and preparation. While we were in that corridor, in that transitional space, nothing could touch us. We were neither what we had been nor what we would become once we reached our destination.

The day before we arrived at the camp, this mood was briefly shattered by the appearance of an enormous wild boar some distance ahead of us on the trail. It was so far from us that even with our binoculars we could barely identify it at first. But despite poor eyesight, wild pigs have prodigious powers of smell, and it began charging us from one hundred yards away. Thundering down the trail toward us . . . yet we still had time to think about what we might do, had drawn our long knives, and in the surveyor's case her assault rifle. Bullets would probably stop a seven-hundred-pound pig, or perhaps not. We did not feel confident taking our attention from the boar to untie the container of handguns from our gear and open its triple locks.

There was no time for the psychologist to prepare any hypnotic suggestion designed to keep us focused and in control; in fact, all she could offer was "Don't get close to it! Don't let it touch you!" while the boar continued to charge. The anthropologist was giggling a bit out of nervousness and the absurdity of experiencing an emergency situation that was taking so long to develop. Only the surveyor had taken direct action: She had dropped to one knee to get a better shot; our orders included the helpful directive to "kill only if you are under threat of being killed."

I was continuing to watch through the binoculars, and as the boar came closer, its face became stranger and stranger. Its features were somehow contorted, as if the beast was dealing with an extreme of inner torment. Nothing about its muzzle or broad, long face looked at all extraordinary, and yet I had the startling impression of some *presence* in the way its gaze seemed turned inward and its head willfully pulled to the left as if there were an invisible bridle. A kind of electricity sparked in its eyes that I could not credit as real. I thought instead it must be a by-product of my now slightly shaky hand on the binoculars.

Whatever was consuming the boar also soon consumed its desire to charge. It veered abruptly leftward, with what I can only describe as a great cry of anguish, into the underbrush. By the time we reached that spot, the boar was gone, leaving behind a thoroughly thrashed trail.

For several hours, my thoughts turned inward toward explanations for what I had seen: parasites and other hitchhikers of a neurological nature. I was searching for entirely rational biological theories. Then, after a time, the boar faded into the backdrop like all else that we had passed on our way from the border, and I was staring into the future again.

The morning after we discovered the tower we rose early, ate our breakfast, and doused our fire. There was a crisp chill to the air common for the season. The surveyor broke open the weapons stash and gave us each a handgun. She herself continued to hold on to the assault rifle; it had the added benefit of a flashlight under the barrel. We had not expected to have to open that particular container so soon, and although none of us protested, I felt a new tension between us. We knew that members of the second expedition to Area X had committed suicide by gunshot and members of the third had shot each other. Not until several subsequent expeditions had suffered zero casualties had our superiors issued firearms again. We were the twelfth expedition.

So we returned to the tower, all four of us. Sunlight came

down dappled through the moss and leaves, created archipelagos of light on the flat surface of the entrance. It remained unremarkable, inert, in no way ominous . . . and yet it took an act of will to stand there, staring at the entry point. I noticed the anthropologist checking her black box, was relieved to see it did not display a glowing red light. If it had, we would have had to abort our exploration, move on to other things. I did not want that, despite the touch of fear.

"How deep do you think it goes down?" the anthropologist asked.

"Remember that we are to put our faith in your measurements," the psychologist answered, with a slight frown. "The measurements do not lie. This structure is 61.4 feet in diameter. It is raised 7.9 inches from the ground. The stairwell appears to have been positioned at or close to due north, which may tell us something about its creation, eventually. It is made of stone and coquina, not of metal or of bricks. These are facts. That it wasn't on the maps means only that a storm may have uncovered the entrance."

I found the psychologist's faith in measurements and her rationalization for the tower's absence from maps oddly . . . endearing? Perhaps she meant merely to reassure us, but I would like to believe she was trying to reassure herself. Her position, to lead and possibly to know more than us, must have been difficult and lonely.

"I hope it's only about six feet deep so we can continue mapping," the surveyor said, trying to be lighthearted, but then she, and we, all recognized the term "six feet under" ghosting through her syntax and a silence settled over us.

"I want you to know that I cannot stop thinking of it as

a *tower*," I confessed. "I can't see it as a tunnel." It seemed important to make the distinction before our descent, even if it influenced their evaluation of my mental state. I saw a tower, plunging into the ground. The thought that we stood at its summit made me a little dizzy.

All three stared at me then, as if I were the strange cry at dusk, and after a moment the psychologist said, grudgingly, "If that helps make you more comfortable, then I don't see the harm."

A silence came over us again, there under the canopy of trees. A beetle spiraled up toward the branches, trailing dust motes. I think we all realized that only now had we truly entered Area X.

"I'll go first and see what's down there," the surveyor said, finally, and we were happy to defer to her.

The initial stairwell curved steeply downward and the steps were narrow, so the surveyor would have to back her way into the tower. We used sticks to clear the spiderwebs as she lowered herself into position on the stairwell. She teetered there, weapon slung across her back, looking up at us. She had tied her hair back and it made the lines of her face seem tight and drawn. Was this the moment when we were supposed to stop her? To come up with some other plan? If so, none of us had the nerve.

With a strange smirk, almost as if judging us, the surveyor descended until we could only see her face framed in the gloom below, and then not even that. She left an empty space that was shocking to me, as if the reverse had actually happened: as if a face had suddenly floated into view out of the darkness. I gasped, which drew a stare from the psychologist. The anthropologist was too busy staring down into the stairwell to notice any of it.

"Is everything okay?" the psychologist called out to the surveyor. Everything had been fine just a second before. Why would anything be different now?

The surveyor made a sharp grunt in answer, as if agreeing with me. For a few moments more, we could still hear the surveyor struggling on those short steps. Then came silence, and then another movement, at a different rhythm, which for a terrifying moment seemed like it might come from a second source.

But then the surveyor called up to us. "Clear to this level!" *This level.* Something within me thrilled to the fact that my vision of a *tower* was not yet disproven.

That was the signal for me to descend with the anthropologist, while the psychologist stood watch. "Time to go," the psychologist said, as perfunctorily as if we were in school and a class was letting out.

An emotion that I could not quite identify surged through me, and for a moment I saw dark spots in my field of vision. I followed the anthropologist so eagerly down through the remains of webs and the embalmed husks of insects into the cool brackishness of that place that I almost tripped her. My last view of the world above: the psychologist peering down at me with a slight frown, and behind her the trees, the blue of the sky almost blinding against the darkness of the sides of the stairwell.

Below, shadows spread across the walls. The temperature dropped and sound became muffled, the soft steps absorbing our tread. Approximately twenty feet beneath the surface, the structure opened out into a lower level. The ceiling was about eight feet high, which meant a good twelve feet of stone lay above us. The flashlight of the surveyor's assault rifle illuminated the space, but she was faced away from us, surveying the walls, which were an off-white and devoid of any adornment. A few cracks indicated either the passage of time or some sudden stressor. The level appeared to be the same circumference as the exposed top, which again supported the idea of a single solid structure buried in the earth.

"It goes farther," the surveyor said, and pointed with her rifle to the far corner, directly opposite the opening where we had come out onto that level. A rounded archway stood there, and a darkness that suggested downward steps. A tower, which made this level not so much a floor as a landing or part of the turret. She started to walk toward the archway while I was still engrossed in examining the walls with my flashlight. Their very blankness mesmerized me. I tried to imagine the builder of this place but could not.

I thought again of the silhouette of the lighthouse, as I had seen it during the late afternoon of our first day at base camp. We assumed that the structure in question was a lighthouse because the map showed a lighthouse at that location and because everyone immediately recognized what a lighthouse *should* look like. In fact, the surveyor and anthropologist had both expressed a kind of *relief* when they had seen the lighthouse. Its appearance on both the map and in reality reassured them, anchored them. Being familiar with its function further reassured them.

With the tower, we knew none of these things. We could not intuit its full outline. We had no sense of its purpose. And now that we had begun to descend into it, the tower *still* failed to reveal any hint of these things. The psychologist might recite the measurements of the "top" of the tower, but those numbers meant nothing, had no wider context. Without context, clinging to those numbers was a form of madness.

"There is a regularity to the circle, seen from the inside walls, that suggests precision in the creation of the building," the anthropologist said. *The building.* Already she had begun to abandon the idea of it being a tunnel.

All of my thoughts came spilling out of my mouth, some final discharge from the state that had overtaken me above. "But what is its *purpose*? And is it believable that it would not be on the maps? Could one of the prior expeditions have built it and hidden it?" I asked all of this and more, not expecting an answer. Even though no threat had revealed itself, it seemed important to eliminate any possible moment of silence. As if somehow the blankness of the walls fed off of silence, and that something might appear in the spaces between our words if we were not careful. Had I expressed this anxiety to the psychologist, she would have been worried, I know. But I was more attuned to solitude than any of us, and I would have characterized that place in that moment of our exploration as watchful.

A gasp from the surveyor cut me off in mid-question, no doubt much to the anthropologist's relief.

"Look!" the surveyor said, training her flashlight down into the archway. We hurried over and stared past her, adding our own illumination.

A stairway did indeed lead down, this time at a gentle curve with much broader steps, but still made of the same materials. At about shoulder height, perhaps five feet high, clinging to the inner wall of the tower, I saw what I first took to be dimly sparkling green vines progressing down into the darkness. I had a sudden absurd memory of the floral wall-paper treatment that had lined the bathroom of my house when I had shared it with my husband. Then, as I stared, the "vines" resolved further, and I saw that they were words, in cursive, the letters raised about six inches off the wall.

"Hold the light," I said, and pushed past them down the first few steps. Blood was rushing through my head again, a roaring confusion in my ears. It was an act of supreme control to walk those few paces. I couldn't tell you what impulse drove me, except that I was the biologist and this looked oddly organic. If the linguist had been there, perhaps I would have deferred to her.

"Don't touch it, whatever it is," the anthropologist warned.

I nodded, but I was too enthralled with the discovery. If I'd had the impulse to touch the words on the wall, I would not have been able to stop myself.

As I came close, did it surprise me that I could under-stand the language the words were written in? Yes. Did it fill me with a kind of elation and dread intertwined? Yes. I tried to suppress the thousand new questions rising up inside of me. In as calm a voice as I could manage, aware of the im-portance of that moment, I read from the beginning, aloud: *"Where lies the strangling fruit that came from the hand of the sinner I shall bring forth the seeds of the dead to share with the worms that . . ."*

Then the darkness took it.

"Words? Words?" the anthropologist said.

Yes, words.

"What are they made of?" the surveyor asked. Did they need to be made of anything?

The illumination cast on the continuing sentence quavered and shook. *Where lies the strangling fruit* became bathed in shadow and in light, as if a battle raged for its meaning.

"Give me a moment. I need to get closer." Did I? Yes, I needed to get closer.

What are they made of?

I hadn't even thought of this, though I should have; I was still trying to parse the lingual meaning, had not transitioned to the idea of taking a physical sample. But what relief at the question! Because it helped me fight the compulsion to keep reading, to descend into the greater darkness and keep descending until I had read all there was to read. Already those initial phrases were infiltrating my mind in unexpected ways, finding fertile ground.

So I stepped closer, peered at *Where lies the strangling fruit*. I saw that the letters, connected by their cursive script, were made from what would have looked to the layperson like rich green fernlike moss but in fact was probably a type of fungi or other eukaryotic organism. The curling filaments were all packed very close together and rising out from the wall. A loamy smell came from the words along with an underlying hint of rotting honey. This miniature forest *swayed*, almost imperceptibly, like sea grass in a gentle ocean current.

Other things existed in this miniature ecosystem. Half-hidden by the green filaments, most of these creatures were translucent and shaped like tiny hands embedded by the base of the palm. Golden nodules capped the fingers on these "hands." I leaned in closer, like a fool, like someone who had not had months of survival training or ever studied biology. Someone tricked into thinking that words should be read.

I was unlucky—or was I lucky? Triggered by a disturbance in the flow of air, a nodule in the W chose that moment to burst open and a tiny spray of golden spores spewed out. I pulled back, but I thought I had felt something enter my nose, experienced a pinprick of escalation in the smell of rotting honey.

Unnerved, I stepped back even farther, borrowing some of the surveyor's best curses, but only in my head. My natural instinct was always for concealment. Already I was imagining the psychologist's reaction to my contamination, if revealed to the group.

"Some sort of fungi," I said finally, taking a deep breath so I could control my voice. "The letters are made from fruiting bodies." Who knew if it were actually true? It was just the closest thing to an answer.

My voice must have seemed calmer than my actual thoughts because there was no hesitation in their response. No hint in their tone of having seen the spores erupt into my face. I had been so close. The spores had been so tiny, so insignificant. *I shall bring forth the seeds of the dead.*

"Words? Made of fungi?" the surveyor said, stupidly echoing me.

"There is no recorded human language that uses this method of writing," the anthropologist said. "Is there any animal that communicates in this way?"

I had to laugh. "No, there is no animal that communicates

in this way." Or, if there were, I could not recall its name, and never did later, either.

"Are you joking? This is a joke, right?" the surveyor said. She looked poised to come down and prove me wrong, but didn't move from her position.

"Fruiting bodies," I replied, almost as if in a trance. "Forming words."

A calm had settled over me. A competing sensation, as if I couldn't breathe, or didn't want to, was clearly psychological not physiological. I had noticed no physical changes, and on some level it didn't matter. I knew it was unlikely we had an antidote to something so unknown waiting back at the camp.

More than anything, the information I was trying to process immobilized me. The words were composed of symbiotic fruiting bodies from a species unknown to me. Second, the dusting of spores on the words meant that the farther down into the tower we explored, the more the air would be full of potential contaminants. Was there any reason to relay this information to the others when it would only alarm them? No, I decided, perhaps selfishly. It was more important to make sure they were not directly exposed until we could come back with the proper equipment. Any other evaluation depended on environmental and biological factors about which I was increasingly convinced I had inadequate data.

I came back up the stairs to the landing. The surveyor and the anthropologist looked expectant, as if I could tell them more. The anthropologist in particular was on edge; her gaze couldn't alight on any one thing but kept moving and moving. Perhaps I could have fabricated information that would have stopped that incessant search. But what could

I tell them about the words on the wall except that they were either impossible or insane, or both? I would have preferred the words be written in an *unknown* language; this would have presented less of a mystery for us to solve, in a way.

"We should go back up," I said. It was not that I recommended this as the best course of action but because I wanted to limit their exposure to the spores until I could see what long-term effects they might have on me. I also knew if I stayed there much longer I might experience a compulsion to go back down the stairs to continue reading the words, and they would have to physically restrain me, and I did not know what I would do then.

There was no argument from the other two. But as we climbed back up, I had a moment of vertigo despite being in such an enclosed space, a kind of panic for a moment, in which the walls suddenly had a fleshy aspect to them, as if we traveled inside of the gullet of a beast.

When we told the psychologist what we had seen, when I recited some of the words, she seemed at first frozen in an oddly attentive way. Then she decided to descend to view the words. I struggled with whether I should warn her against this action. Finally I said, "Only observe from the top of the stairs. We don't know whether there are toxins. When we come back, we should wear breathing masks." These, at least, we had inherited from the last expedition, in a sealed container.

"*Paralysis is not a cogent analysis?*" she said to me with a pointed stare. I felt a kind of itchiness come over me, but I said nothing, did nothing. The others did not even seem to realize she had spoken. It was only later that I realized the psychologist had tried to bind me with a hypnotic suggestion meant for me and me alone.

My reaction apparently fell within the range of acceptable responses, for she descended while we waited anxiously above. What would we do if she did not return? A sense of ownership swept over me. I was agitated by the idea that she might experience the same need to read further and would act upon it. Even though I didn't know what the words meant, I wanted them to mean something so that I might more swiftly remove doubt, bring reason back into all of my equations. Such thoughts distracted me from thinking about the effects of the spores on my system.

Thankfully the other two had no desire to talk as we waited, and after just fifteen minutes the psychologist awkwardly pushed her way up out of the stairwell and into the light, blinking as her vision adjusted.

"Interesting," she said in a flat tone as she loomed over us, wiping the cobwebs from her clothing. "I have never seen anything like that before." She seemed as if she might continue, but then decided against it.

What she had already said verged on the moronic; apparently I was not alone in that assessment.

"Interesting?" the anthropologist said. "No one has ever seen anything like that in the entire history of the world. No one. *Ever.* And you call it *interesting*?" She seemed close to working herself into a bout of hysteria. While the surveyor just stared at both of them as if *they* were the alien organisms.

"Do you need me to calm you?" the psychologist asked. There was a steely tone to her words that made the anthropologist mumble something noncommittal and stare at the ground.

I stepped into the silence with my own suggestion: "We need time to think about this. We need time to decide what to do next." I meant, of course, that I needed time to see if the spores I had inhaled would affect me in a way significant enough to confess to what had happened.

"There may not be enough time in the world for that," the surveyor said. Of all of us, I think she had best grasped the implications of what we had seen: that we might now be living in a kind of nightmare. But the psychologist ignored her and sided with me. "We do need time. We should spend the rest of our day doing what we were sent here to do."

So we returned to camp for lunch and then focused on "ordinary things" while I kept monitoring my body for any changes. Did I feel too cold now, or too hot? Was that ache in my knee from an old injury suffered in the field, or something new? I even checked the black box monitor, but it remained inert. Nothing radical had yet changed in me, and as we took our samples and readings in the general vicinity of the camp—as if to stray too far would be to come under the tower's control—I gradually relaxed and told myself that the spores had had no effect . . . even though I knew that the incubation period for some species could be months or years. I suppose I thought merely that for the next few days at least I might be safe.

The surveyor concentrated on adding detail and nuance to the maps our superiors had given us. The anthropologist went off to examine the remains of some cabins a quarter mile away. The psychologist stayed in her tent, writing in her journal. Perhaps she was reporting on how she was surrounded by idiots, or just setting out every moment of our morning discoveries.

For my part, I spent an hour observing a tiny red-and-green tree frog on the back of a broad, thick leaf and another hour following the path of an iridescent black damselfly that should not have been found at sea level. The rest of the time, I spent up a pine tree, binoculars focused on the coast and the lighthouse. I liked climbing. I also liked the ocean, and I found staring at it had a calming effect. The air was so clean, so fresh, while the world back beyond the border was what it had always been during the modern era: dirty, tired, imperfect, winding down, at war with itself. Back there, I had always felt as if my work amounted to a futile attempt to save us from who we are.

The richness of Area X's biosphere was reflected in the wealth of birdlife, from warblers and flickers to cormorants and black ibis. I could also see a bit into the salt marshes, and my attention there was rewarded by a minute-long glimpse of a pair of otters. At one point, they glanced up and I had a strange sensation that they could see me watching them. It was a feeling I often had when out in the wilderness: that things were not quite what they seemed, and I had to fight against the sensation because it could overwhelm my scientific objectivity. There was also something else, moving ponderously through the reeds, but it was closer to the lighthouse and in deep cover. I could not tell what it was, and after a while its disturbance of the vegetation ceased and I lost track of it entirely. I imagined it might be another wild pig, as they could be good swimmers and were just as omnivorous in their choice of habitats as in their diets.

On the whole, by dusk this strategy of busying ourselves

in our tasks had worked to calm our nerves. The tension lifted somewhat, and we even joked a little bit at dinner. "I wish I knew what you were thinking," the anthropologist confessed to me, and I replied, "No, you don't," which was met with a laughter that surprised me. I didn't want their voices in my head, their ideas of me, nor their own stories or problems. Why would they want mine?

But I did not mind that a sense of camaraderie had begun to take hold, even if it would prove short-lived. The psychologist allowed us each a couple of beers from the store of alcohol, which loosened us up to the point that I even clumsily expressed the idea that we might maintain some sort of contact once we had completed our mission. I had stopped checking myself for physiological or psychological reactions to the spores by then, and found that the surveyor and I got along better than I had expected. I still didn't like the anthropologist very much, but mostly in the context of the mission, not anything she had said to me. I felt that, once in the field, much as some athletes were good in practice and not during the game, she had exhibited a lack of mental toughness thus far. Although just volunteering for such a mission meant something.

When the nightly cry from the marshes came a little after nightfall, while we sat around our fire, we at first called back to it in a drunken show of bravado. The beast in the marshes now seemed like an old friend compared to the tower. We were confident that eventually we would photograph it, document its behavior, tag it, and assign it a place in the taxonomy of living things. It would become known in a way we feared the tower would not. But we stopped calling back when the intensity of its moans heightened in a way that suggested anger, as if it knew we were mocking it. Nervous laughter all around, then, and the psychologist took that as her cue to ready us for the next day.

"Tomorrow we will go back to the tunnel. We will go deeper, taking certain precautions—wearing breathing masks, as suggested. We will record the writing on the walls and get a sense of how old it is, I hope. Also, perhaps a sense of how deep the tunnel descends. In the afternoon, we'll return to our general investigations of the area. We'll repeat this schedule every day until we think we know enough about the tunnel and how it fits into Area X."

Tower, not tunnel. She could have been talking about investigating an abandoned shopping center, for all of the emphasis she put on it . . . and yet something about her tone seemed rehearsed.

Then she abruptly stood and said three words: *"Consolidation of authority."*

Immediately the surveyor and the anthropologist beside me went slack, their eyes unfocused. I was shocked, but I mimicked them, hoping that the psychologist had not noticed the lag. I felt no compulsion whatsoever, but clearly we had been preprogrammed to enter a hypnotic state in response to those words, uttered by the psychologist.

Her demeanor more assertive than just a moment before, the psychologist said, "You will retain a memory of having discussed several options with regard to the tunnel. You will find that you ultimately agreed with me about the best course of action, and that you felt quite confident about this course of action. You will experience a sensation of calm whenever you think about this decision, and you will remain calm once back inside the tunnel, although you will react to any stimuli as per your training. You will not take undue risks.

"You will continue to see a structure that is made of coquina and stone. You will trust your colleagues completely and feel a continued sense of fellowship with them. When you emerge from the structure, any time you see a bird in flight it will trigger a strong feeling that you are doing the *right thing*, that you are in the *right place*. When I snap my fingers, you will have no memory of this conversation, but will follow my directives. You will feel very tired and you will want to retire to your tents to get a good night's sleep before tomorrow's activities. You will not dream. You will not have nightmares."

I stared straight ahead as she said these words, and when she snapped her fingers I took my cue from the actions of the other two. I don't believe the psychologist suspected anything, and I retired to my tent just as the others retired to their tents.

Now I had new data to process, along with the tower. We knew that the psychologist's role was to provide balance and calm in a situation that might become stressful, and that part of this role included hypnotic suggestion. I could not blame her for performing that role. But to see it laid out so nakedly troubled me. It is one thing to think you might be receiving hypnotic suggestion and quite another to experience it as an observer. What level of control could she exert over us? What did she mean by saying that we would continue to think of the tower as made of coquina and stone?

Most important, however, I now could guess at one way in which the spores had affected me: They had made me immune to the psychologist's hypnotic suggestions. They had made me into a kind of conspirator against her. Even if her purposes were benign, I felt a wave of anxiety whenever I thought of confessing that I was resistant to hypnosis—especially since it meant any underlying *conditioning* hidden in our training also was affecting me less and less.

I now hid not one but two secrets, and that meant I was steadily, irrevocably, becoming estranged from the expedition and its purpose.

Estrangement, in all of its many forms, was nothing new for these missions. I understood this from having been given an opportunity along with the others to view videotape of the reentry interviews with the members of the eleventh expedition. Once those individuals had been identified as having returned to their former lives, they were quarantined and questioned about their experiences. Reasonably enough, in most cases family members had called the authorities, finding their loved one's return uncanny or frightening. Any papers found on these returnees had been confiscated by our superiors for examination and study. This information, too, we were allowed to see.

The interviews were fairly short, and in them all eight expedition members told the same story. They had experienced no unusual phenomenon while in Area X, taken no unusual readings, and reported no unusual internal conflicts. But after a period of time, each one of them had had the intense desire to return home and had set out to do so. None of them could explain how they had managed to come back across the border, or why they had gone straight home instead of first reporting to their superiors. One by one they had simply abandoned the expedition, left their journals behind, and drifted home. Somehow.

Throughout these interviews, their expressions were friendly and their gazes direct. If their words seemed a little flat, then this went with the kind of general calm, the almost dreamlike demeanor each had returned with—even the compact, wiry man who had served as that expedition's military expert, a person who'd had a mercurial and energetic personality. In terms of their affect, I could not tell any of the eight apart. I had the sense that they now saw the world through a kind of veil, that they spoke to their interviewers from across a vast distance in time and space.

As for the papers, they proved to be sketches of landscapes within Area X or brief descriptions. Some were cartoons of animals or caricatures of fellow expedition members. All of them had, at some point, drawn the lighthouse or written about it. Looking for hidden meaning in these papers was the same as looking for hidden meaning in the natural world around us. If it existed, it could be activated only by the eye of the beholder.

At the time, I was seeking oblivion, and I sought in those blank, anonymous faces, even the most painfully familiar, a kind of benign escape. A death that would not mean being dead.

02: INTEGRATION

In the morning, I woke with my senses heightened, so that even the rough brown bark of the pines or the ordinary lunging swoop of a woodpecker came to me as a kind of minor revelation. The lingering fatigue from the four-day hike to base camp had left me. Was this some side effect of the spores or just the result of a good night's sleep? I felt so refreshed that I didn't really care.

But my reverie was soon tempered by disastrous news. The anthropologist was gone, her tent empty of her personal effects. Worse, in my view, the psychologist seemed shaken, and as if she hadn't slept. She was squinting oddly, her hair more windblown than usual. I noticed dirt caked on the sides of her boots. She was favoring her right side, as if she had been injured.

"Where is the anthropologist?" the surveyor demanded, while I hung back, trying to make my own sense of it. *What have you done with the anthropologist?* was my unspoken question, which I knew was unfair. The psychologist was no different than she had been before; that I knew the secret to her magician's show did not necessarily mean she was a threat.

The psychologist stepped into our rising panic with a strange assertion: "I talked to her late last night. What she saw in that . . . structure . . . unnerved her to the point that she did not want to continue with this expedition. She has started back to the border to await extraction. She took a partial report with her so that our superiors will know our progress." The psychologist's habit of allowing a slim smile to cross her face at inappropriate times made me want to slap her.

"But she left her gear—her gun, too," the surveyor said.

"She took only what she needed so we would have more—including an extra gun."

"Do you think we need an extra gun?" I asked the psychologist. I was truly curious. In some ways I found the psychologist as fascinating as the tower. Her motivations, her reasons. Why not resort to hypnosis now? Perhaps even with our underlying conditioning some things are not suggestible, or fade with repetition, or she lacked the stamina for it after the events of the night before.

"I think we don't know what we need," the psychologist said. "But we definitely did not need the anthropologist here if she was unable to do her job."

The surveyor and I stared at the psychologist. The surveyor's arms were crossed. We had been trained to keep a close watch on our colleagues for signs of sudden mental stress or dysfunction. She was probably thinking what I was thinking: We had a choice now. We could accept the psychologist's explanation for the anthropologist's disappearance or reject it. If we rejected it, then we were saying the psychologist had lied to us, and therefore also rejecting her authority at a critical time. And if we tried to follow the trail back home, hoping to catch up with the anthropologist, to verify the psychologist's story . . . would we have the will to return to base camp afterward?

"We should continue with our plan," the psychologist said. "We should investigate the . . . tower." The word *tower* in this context felt like a blatant plea for my loyalty.

Still the surveyor wavered, as if fighting the psychologist's suggestion from the night before. This alarmed me in another way. I was not going to leave Area X before investigating the tower. This fact was ingrained in every part of me. And in that context I could not bear to think of losing another member of the team so soon, leaving me alone with the psychologist. Not when I was unsure of her and not when I still had no idea of the effects of my exposure to the spores.

"She's right," I said. "We should continue with the mission. We can make do without the anthropologist." But my pointed stare to the surveyor made it clear to both of them that we would revisit the issue of the anthropologist later.

The surveyor gave a surly nod and looked away.

An audible sigh of either relief or exhaustion came from the psychologist. "That's settled then," she said, and brushed past the surveyor to start making breakfast. The anthropologist had always made breakfast before.

At the tower, the situation changed yet again. The surveyor and I had readied light packs with enough food and water to spend the full day down there. We both had our weapons. We both had donned our breathing masks to keep out the spores, even though it was too late for me. We both wore hard hats with fixed beams on them.

But the psychologist stood on the grass just beyond the circle of the tower, slightly below us, and said, "I'll stand guard here."

"Against what?" I asked, incredulous. I did not want to let the psychologist out of my sight. I wanted her embedded in the risk of the exploration, not standing at the top, with all of the power over us implied by that position.

The surveyor wasn't happy, either. In an almost pleading way that suggested a high level of suppressed stress, she said, "You're supposed to come with us. It's safer with three."

"But you need to know that the entrance is secured," the psychologist said, sliding a magazine into her handgun. The harsh scraping sound echoed more than I would have thought.

The surveyor's grip on her assault rifle tightened until I could see her knuckles whiten. "You need to come down with us."

"There's no *reward in the risk* of all of us going down," the psychologist said, and from the inflection I recognized a hypnotic command.

The surveyor's grip on her rifle loosened. The features of her face became somehow indistinct for a moment.

"You're right," the surveyor said. "Of course, you're right. It makes perfect sense."

A twinge of fear traveled down my back. Now it was two against one.

I thought about that for a moment, took in the full measure of the psychologist's stare as she focused her attention on me. Nightmarish, paranoid scenarios came to me. Returning to find the entrance blocked, or the psychologist picking us off as we reached for the open sky. Except: She could have killed us in our sleep any night of the week.

"It's not that important," I said after a moment. "You're as valuable to us up here as down there."

And so we descended, as before, under the psychologist's watchful eye.

The first thing I noticed on the staging level before we reached the wider staircase that spiraled down, before we encountered again the words written on the wall . . . the tower was *breathing*. The tower *breathed*, and the walls when I went to touch them carried the echo of a heartbeat . . . and they were not made of stone but of *living tissue*. Those walls were still blank, but a kind of silvery-white phosphorescence rose off of them. The world seemed to lurch, and I sat down heavily next to the wall, and the surveyor was by my side, trying to help me up. I think I was shaking as I finally stood. I don't know if I can convey the enormity of that moment in words. The tower was a living creature of some sort. *We were descending into an organism.*

"What's wrong?" the surveyor was asking me, voice muffled through her mask. "What happened?"

I grabbed her hand, forced her palm against the wall.

"Let me go!" She tried to pull away, but I kept her there.

"Do you feel that?" I asked, unrelenting. "Can you feel that?"

"Feel *what*? What are you talking about?" She was scared, of course. To her, I was acting irrationally.

Still, I persisted: "A vibration. A kind of beat." I removed my hand from hers, stepped back.

The surveyor took a long, deep breath, and kept her hand on the wall. "No. Maybe. No. No, nothing."

"What about the wall. What is it made of?"

"Stone, of course," she said. In the arc of my helmet flashlight, her shadowed face was hollowed out, her eyes large and circled by darkness, the mask making it look like she had no nose or mouth.

I took a deep breath. I wanted it all to spill out: that I had been contaminated, that the psychologist was hypnotizing us far more than we might have suspected. *That the walls were made of living tissue.* But I didn't. Instead, I "got my shit together," as my husband used to say. I got my shit together because we were going to go forward and the surveyor couldn't see what I saw, couldn't experience what I was experiencing. And I couldn't make her see it.

"Forget it," I said. "I became disoriented for a second."

"Look, we should go back up now. You're panicking," the surveyor said. We had all been told we might see things that weren't there while in Area X. I know she was thinking that this had happened to me.

I held up the black box on my belt. "Nope—it's not flashing. We're good." It was a joke, a feeble joke, but still.

"You saw something that wasn't there." She wasn't going to let me off the hook.

You can't see what is *there,* I thought.

"Maybe," I admitted, "but isn't that important, too? Isn't that part of all of this? The reporting? And something I see that you don't might be important."

The surveyor weighed that for a moment. "How do you feel now?"

"I feel fine," I lied. "I don't see anything now," I lied. My heart felt like an animal had become trapped in my chest and was trying to crawl out. The surveyor was now surrounded by a corona of the white phosphorescence from the walls. Nothing was receding. Nothing was leaving me.

"Then we'll go on," the surveyor said. "But only if you promise to tell me if you see anything unusual again."

I almost laughed at that, I remember. *Unusual?* Like strange words on a wall? Written among tiny communities of creatures of unknown origin.

"I promise," I said. "And you will do the same for me, right?" Turning the tables, making her realize it might happen to her, too.

She said, "Just don't touch me again or I'll hurt you."

I nodded in agreement. She didn't like knowing I was physically stronger than her.

Under the terms of that flawed agreement we proceeded to the stairs and into the gullet of the tower, the depths now revealing themselves in a kind of ongoing horror show of such beauty and biodiversity that I could not fully take it all in. But I tried, just as I had always tried, even from the very beginning of my career.

My lodestone, the place I always thought of when people asked me why I became a biologist, was the overgrown swimming pool in the backyard of the rented house where I grew up. My mother was an overwrought artist who achieved some success but was a little too fond of alcohol and always struggled to find new clients, while my dad the underemployed accountant specialized in schemes to get rich quick that usually brought in nothing. Neither of them seemed to possess the ability to focus on one thing for any length of time. Sometimes it felt as if I had been placed with a family rather than born into one.

They did not have the will or inclination to clean the kidney-shaped pool, even though it was fairly small. Soon after we moved in, the grass around its edges grew long. Sedge weeds and other towering plants became prevalent. The short bushes lining the fence around the pool lunged up to obscure the chain link. Moss grew in the cracks in the tile path that circled it. The water level slowly rose, fed by the rain, and the surface became more and more brackish with algae. Dragonflies continually scouted the area. Bullfrogs moved in, the wriggling malformed dots of their tadpoles always present. Water gliders and aquatic beetles began to make the place their own. Rather than get rid of my thirty-gallon freshwater aquarium, as my parents wanted, I dumped the fish into the pool, and some survived the shock of that. Local birds, like herons and egrets, began to appear, drawn by the frogs and fish and insects. By some miracle, too, small turtles began to live in the pool, although I had no idea how they had gotten there.

Within months of our arrival, the pool had become a functioning ecosystem. I would slowly enter through the creaking wooden gate and observe it all from a rusty lawn chair I had set up in a far corner. Despite a strong and well-founded fear of drowning, I had always loved being around bodies of water.

Inside the house, my parents did whatever banal, messy things people in the human world usually did, some of it loudly. But I could easily lose myself in the microworld of the pool.

Inevitably my focus netted from my parents useless lectures of worry over my chronic introversion, as if by doing so they could convince me they were still in charge. I didn't have enough (or any) friends, they reminded me. I didn't seem to make the effort. I could be earning money from a part-time job. But when I told them that several times, like a reluctant ant lion, I had had to hide from bullies at the bottom of the gravel pits that lay amid the abandoned fields beyond the school, they had no answers. Nor when one day for "no reason" I punched a fellow student in the face when she said hello to me in the lunch line.

So we proceeded, locked into our separate imperatives. They had their lives, and I had mine. I liked most of all pretending to be a biologist, and pretending often leads to becoming a reasonable facsimile of what you mimic, even if only from a distance. I wrote down my pool observations in several journals. I knew each individual frog from the next, Old Flopper so much different from Ugly Leaper, and during which month I could expect the grass to teem with hopping juveniles. I knew which species of heron turned up year-round and which were migrants. The beetles and dragonflies were harder to identify, their life cycles harder to intuit, but I still diligently tried to understand them. In all of this, I eschewed books on ecology or biology. I wanted to discover the information on my own first.

As far as I was concerned—an only child, and an expert in the uses of solitude—my observations of this miniature paradise could have continued forever. I even jury-rigged a waterproof light to a waterproof camera and planned to submerge the contraption beneath the dark surface, to snap pictures using a long wire attached to the camera button. I have no idea if it would have worked, because suddenly I didn't have the luxury of time. Our luck ran out, and we couldn't afford the rent anymore. We moved to a tiny apartment, stuffed full of my mother's paintings, which all resembled wallpaper to me. One of the great traumas of my life was worrying about the pool. Would the new owners see the beauty and the importance of leaving it as is, or would they destroy it, create unthinking slaughter in honor of the pool's real function?

I never found out—I couldn't bear to go back, even if I also could never forget the richness of that place. All I could do was look forward, apply what I had learned from watching the inhabitants of the pool. And I never did look back, for better or worse. If funding for a project ran out, or the area we studied was suddenly bought for development, I never returned. There are certain kinds of deaths that one should not be expected to relive, certain kinds of connections so deep that when they are broken you feel the snap of the link inside you.

As we descended into the tower, I felt again, for the first time in a long time, the flush of discovery I had experienced as a child. But I also kept waiting for the snap.

Where lies the strangling fruit that came from the hand of the sinner I shall bring forth the seeds of the dead to share with the worms that . . .

ANNIHILATION

The tower steps kept revealing themselves, those whitish steps like the spiraling teeth of some unfathomable beast, and we kept descending because there seemed to be no choice. I wished at times for the blinkered seeing of the surveyor. I knew now why the psychologist had sheltered us, and I wondered how she withstood it, for she had no one to shield her from . . . anything.

At first, there were "merely" the words, and that was enough. They occurred always at roughly the same level against the left-hand side of the wall, and for a time I tried to record them, but there were too many of them and the sense of them came and went, so that to follow the meaning of the words was to follow a trail of deception. That was one agreement the surveyor and I came to right away: that we would document the physicality of the words, but that it would require a separate mission, another day, to photograph that continuous, never-ending sentence.

. . . to share with the worms that gather in the darkness and surround the world with the power of their lives while from the dim-lit halls of other places forms that never could be writhe for the impatience of the few who have never seen or been seen . . .

The sense of unease in ignoring the ominous quality of those words was palpable. It infected our own sentences when we spoke, as we tried to catalogue the biological reality of what we were *both* seeing. Either the psychologist wanted us to see the words and how they were written or simply suppressing the physical reality of the tower's walls was a monumental and exhausting task.

These things, too, we experienced together during our initial descent into the darkness: The air became cooler but also damp, and with the drop in temperature came a kind of gentle sweetness, as of a muted nectar. We also both saw the tiny hand-shaped creatures that lived among the words. The ceilings were higher than we would have guessed, and by the light of our helmets as we looked up, the surveyor could see glints and whorls as of the trails of snails or slugs. Little tufts of moss or lichen dotted that ceiling, and, exhibiting great tensile strength, tiny long-limbed translucent creatures that resembled cave shrimp stilt-walked there as well.

Things only I could see: That the walls minutely rose and fell with the tower's breathing. That the colors of the words shifted in a rippling effect, like the strobing of a squid. That, with a variation of about three inches above the current words and three inches below, there existed a ghosting of *prior words*, written in the same cursive script. Effectively, these layers of words formed a watermark, for they were just an impression against the wall, a pale hint of green or sometimes purple the only sign that once they might have been raised letters. Most seemed to repeat the main thread, but some did not.

For a time, while the surveyor took photographic samples of the living words, I read the phantom words to see how they might deviate. It was hard to read them—there were several overlapping strands that started and stopped and started up again. I easily lost track of individual words and phrases. The number of such ghost scripts faded into the wall suggested this process had been ongoing for a long time. Although without some sense of the length of each "cycle," I could not give even a rough estimate in years.

There was another element to the communications on

the wall, too. One I wasn't sure if the surveyor could see or not. I decided to test her.

"Do you recognize this?" I asked the surveyor, pointing to a kind of interlocking latticework that at first I hadn't even realized was a pattern but that covered the wall from just below the phantom scripts to just above them, the main strand roughly in the middle. It vaguely resembled scorpions strung end-to-end arising, only to be subsumed again. I didn't even know if I was looking at a language, per se. It could have been a decorative pattern for all I knew.

Much to my relief, she could see it. "No, I don't recognize it," she said. "But I'm not an expert."

I felt a surge of irritation, but it wasn't directed at her. I had the wrong brain for this task, and so did she; we needed a linguist. We could look at that latticework script for ages and the most original thought I would have is that it resembled the sharp branching of hard coral. To the surveyor it might resemble the rough tributaries of a vast river.

Eventually, though, I was able to reconstruct fragments of a handful of some of the variants: *Why should I rest when wickedness exists in the world . . . God's love shines on anyone who understands the limits of endurance, and allows forgiveness . . . Chosen for the service of a higher power.* If the main thread formed a kind of dark, incomprehensible sermon, then the fragments shared an affinity with that purpose without the heightened syntax.

Did they come from longer accounts of some sort, possibly from members of prior expeditions? If so, for what purpose? And over how many years?

But all such questions would be for later, in the light of

the surface. Mechanically, like a golem, I just took photographs of key phrases—even as the surveyor thought I was clicking pictures of blank wall, or off-center shots of the main fungal words—to put some distance between myself and whatever I might think about these variants. While the main scrawl continued, and continued to unnerve: . . . *in the black water with the sun shining at midnight, those fruit shall come ripe and in the darkness of that which is golden shall split open to reveal the revelation of the fatal softness in the earth* . . .

Those words defeated me somehow. I took samples as we went, but halfheartedly. All of these tiny remnants I was stuffing into glass tubes with tweezers . . . what would they tell me? Not much, I felt. Sometimes you get a sense of when the truth of things will not be revealed by microscopes. Soon, too, the sound of the heartbeat through the walls became so loud to me I stopped to put in earplugs to muffle its beat, choosing a moment while the surveyor's attention lay elsewhere. Be-masked, half-deaf for different reasons, we continued our descent.

It should have been me who noticed the change, not her. But after an hour of downward progress, the surveyor stopped on the steps below me.

"Do you think the words on the wall are becoming . . . fresher?"

"Fresher?"

"More recent."

I just stared at her for a moment. I had become acclimated to the situation, had done my best to pretend to be the kind of impartial observer who simply catalogues details. But I felt all of that hard-won distance slipping away.

"Turn off your light?" I suggested, as I did the same.

The surveyor hesitated. After my show of impulsiveness earlier, it would be some time before she trusted me again. Not the kind of trust that responded unthinkingly to a request to plunge us into darkness. But she did it. The truth was, I had purposefully left my gun in its belt holster and she could have extinguished me in a moment with her assault rifle, with one fluid motion pulling on the strap and freeing it from her shoulder. This premonition of violence made little rational sense, and yet it came to me too easily, almost as if placed in my mind by outside forces.

In the dark, as the tower's heartbeat still throbbed against my eardrums, the letters, the words, swayed as the walls trembled with their breathing, and I saw that indeed the words seemed more active, the colors brighter, the strobing more intense than I remembered it from levels above. It was an even more noticeable effect than if the words had been written in ink with a fountain pen. *The bright, wet slickness of the new.*

Standing there in that impossible place, I said it before the surveyor could, to own it.

"Something below us is writing this script. Something below us may still be in the process of writing this script." We were exploring an organism that might contain a mysterious second organism, which was itself using yet other organisms to write words on the wall. It made the overgrown pool of my youth seem simplistic, one-dimensional.

We turned our lights back on. I saw fear in the surveyor's

eyes, but also a strange determination. I have no idea what she saw in me.

"Why did you say something?" she asked.

I didn't understand.

"Why did you say 'something' rather than 'someone'? Why can't it be 'someone'?"

I just shrugged.

"Get out your gun," the surveyor said, a hint of disgust in her voice masking some deeper emotion.

I did as I was told because it didn't really matter to me. But holding the gun made me feel clumsy and odd, as if it were the wrong reaction to what might confront us.

Whereas I had taken the lead to this point, now it seemed as if we had switched roles, and the nature of our exploration changed as a result. Apparently, we had just established a new protocol. We stopped documenting the words and organisms on the wall. We walked much more swiftly, our attention focused on interpreting the darkness in front of us. We spoke in whispers, as if we might be overheard. I went first, with the surveyor covering me from behind until the curves, where she went first and I followed. At no point did we speak of turning back. The psychologist watching over us might as well have been thousands of miles away. We were charged with the nervous energy of knowing there might be some answer below us. A living, breathing answer.

At least, the surveyor *may* have thought of it in those terms. She couldn't feel or hear the beating of the walls. But as we progressed, even I could not see the writer of those words in my mind. All I could see was what I had seen when I had stared back at the border on our way to base camp: a fuzzy white blankness. Yet still I knew it could not be human.

Why? For a very good reason—one the surveyor finally noticed another twenty minutes into our descent.

"There's something on the floor," she said.

Yes, there was something on the floor. For a long time now, the steps had been covered in a kind of residue. I hadn't stopped to examine it because I hadn't wanted to unnerve the surveyor, uncertain if she would ever come to see it. The residue covered a distance from the edge of the left wall to about two feet from the right wall. This meant it filled a space on the steps about eight or nine feet wide.

"Let me take a look," I said, ignoring her quivering finger. I knelt, turning to train my helmet light on the upper steps behind me. The surveyor walked up to stare over my shoulder. The residue sparkled with a kind of subdued golden shimmer shot through with flakes red like dried blood. It seemed partially reflective. I probed it with a pen.

"It's slightly viscous, like slime," I said. "And about half an inch deep over the steps."

The overall impression was of something *sliding* down the stairs.

"What about those marks?" the surveyor asked, leaning forward to point again. She was whispering, which seemed useless to me, and her voice had a catch in it. But every time I noticed her becoming more panicky, I found it made me calmer.

I studied the marks for a moment. Sliding, perhaps, or *dragged*, but slowly enough to reveal much more in the residue left behind. The marks she had pointed to were oval, and about a foot long by half a foot wide. Six of them were splayed over the steps, in two rows. A flurry of indentations inside these shapes resembled the marks left by cilia. About ten inches outside of these tracks, encircling them, were two lines. This irregular double circle undulated out and then in again, almost like the hem of a skirt. Beyond this "hem" were faint indicators of further "waves," as of some force emanating from a central body that had left a mark. It resembled most closely the lines left in sand as the surf recedes during low tide. Except that something had blurred the lines and made them fuzzy, like charcoal drawings.

This discovery fascinated me. I could not stop staring at the trail, the cilia marks. I imagined such a creature might correct for the slant of the stairs much like a geo-stabilizing camera would correct for bumps in a track.

"Have you ever seen anything like that?" the surveyor asked.

"No," I replied. With an effort, I bit back a more caustic response. "No, I never have." Certain trilobites, snails, and worms left trails simple by comparison but vaguely similar. I was confident no one back in the world had ever seen a trail this complex or this large.

"What about *that*?" The surveyor indicated a step a little farther up.

I trained a light on it and saw a suggestion of a boot print in the residue. "Just one of our own boots." So mundane in comparison. So boring.

The light on her helmet shuddered from side to side as she shook her head. "No. See."

She pointed out my boot prints and hers. This imprint was from a third set, and headed back up the steps.

"You're right," I said. "That's another person, down here not long ago."

The surveyor started cursing.

At the time, we didn't think to look for more sets of boot prints.

According to the records we had been shown, the first expedition reported nothing unusual in Area X, just pristine, empty wilderness. After the second and third expeditions did not return, and their fate became known, the expeditions were shut down for a time. When they began again, it was using carefully chosen volunteers who might at least know a measure of the full risk. Since then, some expeditions had been more successful than others.

The eleventh expedition in particular had been difficult—and personally difficult for me with regard to a fact about which I have not been entirely honest thus far.

My husband was on the eleventh expedition as a medic. He had never wanted to be a doctor, had always wanted to be in first response or working in trauma. "A triage nurse in the field," as he put it. He had been recruited for Area X by a friend, who remembered him from when they had both worked for the navy, before he switched over to ambulance service. At first he hadn't said yes, had been unsure, but over time they convinced him. It caused a lot of strife between us, although we already had many difficulties.

I know this information might not be hard for anyone to find out, but I have hoped that in reading this account, you might find me a credible, objective witness. Not someone who volunteered for Area X because of some other event unconnected to the purpose of the expeditions. And, in a sense, this is still true, and my husband's status as a member of an expedition is in many ways irrelevant to why I signed up.

But how could I not be affected by Area X, if only through him? One night, about a year after he had headed for the border, as I lay alone in bed, I heard someone in the kitchen. Armed with a baseball bat, I left the bedroom and turned on all the lights in the house. I found my husband next to the refrigerator, still dressed in his expedition clothes, drinking milk until it flowed down his chin and neck. Eating leftovers furiously.

I was speechless. I could only stare at him as if he were a mirage and if I moved or said anything he would dissipate into nothing, or less than nothing.

We sat in the living room, him on the sofa and me in a chair opposite. I needed some distance from this sudden apparition. He did not remember how he had left Area X, did not remember the journey home at all. He had only the vaguest recollection of the expedition itself. There was an odd calm about him, punctured only by moments of remote panic when, in asking him what had happened, he recognized that his amnesia was unnatural. Gone from him, too, seemed to be any memory of how our marriage had begun to disintegrate well before our arguments over his leaving for Area X. He contained within him now the very distance he had in so many subtle and not so subtle ways accused me of in the past.

After a time, I couldn't take it any longer. I took off his clothes, made him shower, then led him into the bedroom and made love to him with me on top. I was trying to reclaim remnants of the man I remembered, the one who, so unlike me, was outgoing and impetuous and always wanted to be of use. The man who had been a passionate recreational sailor, and for two weeks out of the year went with friends to the coast to go boating. I could find none of that in him now.

The whole time he was inside me he looked up at my face with an expression that told me he did remember me but only through a kind of fog. It helped for a while, though. It made him more real, allowed me to pretend.

But only for a while. I only had him in my life again for about twenty-four hours. They came for him the next evening, and once I went through the long, drawn-out process of receiving security clearance, I visited him in the observation facility right up until the end. That antiseptic place where they tested him and tried without success to break through both his calm and his amnesia. He would greet me like an old friend—an anchor of sorts, to make sense of his existence—but not like a lover. I confess I went because I had hopes that there remained some spark of the man I'd once known. But I never really found it. Even the day I was told he had been diagnosed with inoperable, systemic cancer, my husband stared at me with a slightly puzzled expression on his face.

He died six months later. During all that time, I could never get beyond the mask, could never find the man I had known inside of him. Not through my personal interactions with him, not through eventually watching the interviews with him and the other members of the expedition, all of whom died of cancer as well.

Whatever had happened in Area X, he had not come back. Not really.

Ever farther down into the darkness we went, and I had to ask myself if any of this had been experienced by my husband. I did not know how my infection changed things. Was I on the same journey, or had he found something completely different? If similar, how had his reactions been different, and how had that changed what happened next?

The path of slime grew thicker and we could now tell that the red flecks were living organisms discharged by whatever lay below, for they wriggled in the viscous layer. The color of the substance had intensified so that it resembled a sparkling golden carpet set out for us to tread upon on our way to some strange yet magnificent banquet.

"Should we go back?" the surveyor would say, or I would say.

And the other would say, "Just around the next corner. Just a little farther, and then we will go back." It was a test of a fragile trust. It was a test of our curiosity and fascination, which walked side by side with our fear. A test of whether we preferred to be ignorant or unsafe. The feel of our boots as we advanced step by careful step through that viscous discharge, the way in which the stickiness seemed to mire us even as we managed to keep moving, would eventually end in inertia, we knew. If we pushed it too far.

But then the surveyor rounded a corner ahead of me

and recoiled into me, shoved me back up the steps, and I let her.

"There's something down there," she whispered in my ear. "Something like a body or a person."

I didn't point out that a body could be a person. "Is it writing words on the wall?"

"No—*slumped down* by the side of the wall. I only caught a glimpse." Her breathing came quick and shallow against her mask.

"A man or a woman?" I asked.

"I *thought* it was a person," she said, ignoring my question. "I thought it was a person. I thought it was." Bodies were one thing; no amount of training could prepare you for encountering a monster.

But we could not climb back out of the tower without first investigating this new mystery. We could not. I grabbed her by the shoulders, made her look at me. "You said it's like a person sitting down against the side of the wall. That's *not* whatever we've been tracking. This has to do with the *other boot print*. You know that. We can risk taking a look at whatever this is, and then we will go back up. This is as far as we go, no matter what we find, I promise."

The surveyor nodded. The idea of this being the extent of it, of not going farther down, was enough to steady her. *Just get through this last thing, and you'll see the sunlight soon.*

We started back down. The steps seemed particularly slippery now, even though it might have been our jitters, and we walked slowly, using the blank slate of the right wall to keep our balance. The tower was silent, holding its breath, its heartbeat suddenly slow and far more distant than before, or perhaps I could only hear the blood rushing through my head.

Turning the corner, I saw the figure and shone my helmet light on it. If I'd hesitated a second longer, I never would have had the nerve. It was the body of the anthropologist, slumped against the left-hand wall, her hands in her lap, her head down as if in prayer, something green spilling out from her mouth. Her clothing seemed oddly fuzzy, indistinct. A faint golden glow arose from her body, almost imperceptible; I imagined the surveyor could not see it at all. In no scenario could I imagine the anthropologist alive. All I could think was, *The psychologist lied to us,* and suddenly the pressure of her presence far above, guarding the entrance, was pressing down on me in an intolerable way.

I put out a palm to the surveyor, indicating that she should stay where she was, behind me, and I stepped forward, light pointed down into the darkness. I walked past the body far enough to confirm the stairs below were empty, then hurried back up.

"Keep watch while I take a look at the body," I said. I didn't tell her I had sensed a faint, echoing suggestion of *something* much farther below, moving slowly.

"It *is* a body?" the surveyor said. Perhaps she had expected something far stranger. Perhaps she thought the figure was just sleeping.

"It's the anthropologist," I said, and saw that information register in the tensing of her shoulders. Without another word, she brushed past me to take up a position just beyond the body, assault rifle aimed into the darkness.

Gently, I knelt beside the anthropologist. There wasn't

much left of her face, and odd burn marks were all over the remaining skin. Spilling out from her broken jaw, which looked as though someone had wrenched it open in a single act of brutality, was a torrent of green ash that sat on her chest in a mound. Her hands, palms up in her lap, had no skin left on them, only a kind of gauzy filament and more burn marks. Her legs seemed fused together and half-melted, one boot missing and one flung against the wall. Strewn around the anthropologist were some of the same sample tubes I had brought with me. Her black box, crushed, lay several feet from her body.

"What happened to her?" the surveyor whispered. She kept taking quick, nervous glances back at me as she stood guard, almost as if whatever had happened wasn't over. As if she expected the anthropologist to come back to horrifying life.

I didn't answer her. All I could have said was *I don't know,* a sentence that was becoming a kind of witness to our own ignorance or incompetence. Or both.

I shone my light on the wall above the anthropologist. For several feet, the script on the wall became erratic, leaping up and dipping down, before regaining its equilibrium.

. . . the shadows of the abyss are like the petals of a monstrous flower that shall blossom within the skull and expand the mind beyond what any man can bear . . .

"I think she interrupted the creator of the script on the wall," I said.

"And it did that to her?" She was pleading with me to find some other explanation.

I didn't have one, so I didn't reply, just went back to observing as she stood there, watching me.

A biologist is not a detective, but I began to think like a detective. I surveyed the ground to all sides, identifying first my own boot prints on the steps and then the surveyor's. We had obscured the original tracks, but you could still see traces. First of all, the *thing*—and no matter what the surveyor might hope, I could not think of it as human— had clearly turned in a frenzy. Instead of the smooth sliding tracks, the slime residue formed a kind of clockwise swirl, the marks of the "feet," as I thought of them, elongated and narrowed by the sudden change. But on top of this swirl, I could also see boot prints. I retrieved the one boot, being careful to walk around the edges of the evidence of the encounter. The boot prints in the middle of the swirl were indeed from the anthropologist—and I could follow partial imprints back up the right-hand side of the wall, as if she had been hugging it.

An image began to form in my mind, of the anthropologist creeping down in the dark to observe the creator of the script. The glittering glass tubes strewn around her body made me think that she had hoped to take a sample. But how insane or oblivious! Such a risk, and the anthropologist had never struck me as impulsive or brave. I stood there for a moment, and then backtracked even farther up the stairs as I motioned to the surveyor, much to her distress, to hold her position. Perhaps if there had been something to shoot she would have been calmer, but we were left with only what lingered in our imaginations.

Another dozen steps up, right where you could still have a slit of a view of the dead anthropologist, I found two sets of boot prints, facing each other. One set belonged to the anthropologist. The other was neither mine nor the surveyor's.

Something clicked into place, and I could see it all in my head. In the middle of the night, the psychologist had woken the anthropologist, put her under hypnosis, and together they had come to the tower and climbed down this far. At this point, the psychologist had given the anthropologist an order, under hypnosis, one that she probably knew was suicidal, and the anthropologist had walked right up to the thing that was writing the words on the wall and tried to take a sample—and died trying, probably in agony. The psychologist had then fled; certainly, as I walked back down I could find no trace of her boot prints below that point.

Was it pity or empathy that I felt for the anthropologist? Weak, trapped, with no choice.

The surveyor waited for me, anxious. "What did you find?"

"Another person was here with the anthropologist." I told the surveyor my theory.

"But why would the psychologist do that?" she asked me. "We were going to all come down here in the morning anyway."

I felt as if I were observing the surveyor from a thousand miles away.

"I have no idea," I said, "but she has been hypnotizing all of us, and not just to give us peace of mind. Perhaps this expedition had a different purpose than what we were told."

"Hypnotism." She said the word like it was meaningless. "How do you know that? How could you possibly know that?" The surveyor seemed resentful—of me or of the theory, I couldn't tell which. But I could understand why.

"Because, somehow, I have become impervious to it," I told her. "She hypnotized you before we came down here today, to make sure you would do your duty. I saw her do it." I wanted to confess to the surveyor—to tell her *how* I had become impervious—but believed that that would be a mistake.

"And you did *nothing*? If this is even true." At least she was considering the possibility of believing me. Perhaps some residue, some fuzziness, from the episode had stuck in her mind.

"I didn't want the psychologist to know that she couldn't hypnotize me." And, I had *wanted* to come down here.

The surveyor stood there for a moment, considering.

"Believe me or don't believe me," I said. "But believe this: When we go up there, we need to be ready for anything. We may need to restrain or kill the psychologist because we don't know what she's planning."

"Why would she be planning anything?" the surveyor asked. Was that disdain in her voice or just fear again?

"Because she must have different orders than the ones we got," I said, as if explaining to a child.

When she did not reply, I took that as a sign that she was beginning to acclimate to the idea.

"I'll need to go first, because she can't affect me. And you'll need to wear these. It might help you resist the hypnotic suggestion." I gave her my extra set of earplugs.

She took them hesitantly. "No," she said. "We'll go up together, at the same time."

"That isn't wise," I said.

"I don't care what it is. You're not going up top without me. I'm not waiting there in the dark for you to fix everything."

I thought about that for a moment, then said, "Fine. But if I see that she is starting to coerce you, I'll have to stop her." Or at least try.

"If you're right," the surveyor said. "If you're telling the truth."

"I am."

She ignored me, said, "What about the body?"

Did that mean we were agreed? I hoped so. Or maybe she would try to disarm me on the way up. Perhaps the psychologist had already prepared her in this regard.

"We leave the anthropologist here. We can't be weighed down, and we also don't know what contaminants we might bring with us."

The surveyor nodded. At least she wasn't sentimental. There was nothing left of the anthropologist in that body, and we both knew it. I was trying very hard not to think of the anthropologist's last moments alive, of the terror she must have felt as she continued trying to perform a task that she had been willed to do by another, even though it meant her own death. *What had she seen? What had she been looking at before it all went dark?*

Before we turned back, I took one of the glass tubes strewn around the anthropologist. It contained just a trace of a thick, fleshlike substance that gleamed darkly golden. Perhaps she had gotten a useful sample after all, near the end.

As we ascended toward the light, I tried to distract myself. I kept reviewing my training over and over again, searching for a clue, for any scrap of information that might lead to some revelation about our discoveries. But I could find nothing, could only wonder at my own gullibility in thinking that I had been told anything at all of use. Always, the emphasis was on our own capabilities and knowledge base. Always, as I looked back, I could see that there had been an almost willful intent to obscure, to misdirect, disguised as concern that we not be frightened or overwhelmed.

The map had been the first form of misdirection, for what was a map but a way of emphasizing some things and making other things invisible? Always, we were directed to the map, to memorizing the details on the map. Our instructor, who remained nameless to us, drilled us for six long months on the position of the lighthouse relative to the base camp, the number of miles from one ruined patch of houses to another. The number of miles of coastline we would be expected to explore. Almost always in the context of the *lighthouse*, not the base camp. We became so comfortable with that map, with the dimensions of it, and the thought of what it contained that it stopped us from asking *why* or even *what*.

Why this stretch of coast? *What* might lie inside the lighthouse? *Why* was the camp set back into the forest, far from the lighthouse but fairly close to the tower (which, of course, did not exist on the map)—and had the base camp always been there? *What* lay beyond the map? Now that I knew the extent of the hypnotic suggestion that had been used on us, I realized that the focus on the map might have itself been an embedded cue. That if we did not ask questions, it was because we were programmed not to ask questions. That the lighthouse, representative or actual, might have been a subconscious trigger for a hypnotic suggestion—and that it might also have been the epicenter of whatever had spread out to become Area X.

My briefing on the ecology of that place had had a similar blinkered focus. I had spent most of my time becoming familiar with the natural transitional ecosystems, with the flora and fauna and the cross-pollination I could expect to find. But I'd also had an intense refresher on fungi and lichen that, in light of the words on the wall, now stood out in my mind as being the true purpose of all of that study. If the map had been meant solely to distract, then the ecology research had been meant, after all, to truly prepare me. Unless I was being paranoid. But if I wasn't, it meant they knew about the tower, perhaps had always known about the tower.

From there, my suspicions grew. They had put us through grueling survival and weapons training, so grueling that most evenings we went right to sleep in our separate quarters. Even on those few occasions when we trained together, we were training apart. They took away our names in the second month, stripped them from us. The only names applied to things in Area X, and only in terms of their most general label. This, too, a kind of distraction from asking certain questions that could only be reached through knowing specific details. But the *right* specific details, not, for example, that there were six species of poisonous snakes in Area X. A reach, yes, but I was not in the mood to set aside even the most unlikely scenarios.

By the time we were ready to cross the border, we knew everything . . . and we knew nothing.

The psychologist wasn't there when we emerged, blinking into the sunlight, ripping off our masks and breathing in the fresh air. We had been ready for almost any scenario, but not for the psychologist's absence. It left us adrift for a while, afloat in that ordinary day, the sky so brightly blue, the stand of trees casting long shadows. I took out my earplugs and found I couldn't hear the beating of the tower's heartbeat at all. How what we had seen below could coexist with the mundane was baffling. It was as if we had come up too fast from a deep-sea dive but it was the memories of the creatures we had seen that had given us the bends. We just kept searching the environs for the psychologist, certain she was hiding, and half-hoping we would find her, because surely she had an explanation. It was, after a time, pathological to keep searching the same area around the tower. But for almost an hour we could not find a way to stop.

Finally I could not deny the truth.

"She's gone," I said.

"Maybe she's back at the base camp," the surveyor said.

"Would you agree that her absence is a sign of guilt?" I asked.

The surveyor spat into the grass, regarded me closely. "No, I would not. Maybe something happened to her. Maybe she needed to go back to the camp."

"You saw the footprints. You saw the body."

She motioned with her rifle. "Let's just get back to base camp."

I couldn't read her at all. I didn't know if she was turning on me or just cautious. Coming up aboveground had emboldened her, regardless, and I had preferred her uncertain.

But back at base camp, some of her resolve crumbled again. The psychologist wasn't there. Not only wasn't she there, but she had taken half of our supplies and most of the guns. Either that or buried them somewhere. So we knew the psychologist was still alive.

You must understand how I felt then, how the surveyor must have felt: We were scientists, trained to observe natural phenomena and the results of human activity. We had not been trained to encounter what appeared to be the uncanny. In unusual situations there can be a comfort in the presence of even someone you think might be your enemy. Now we had come close to the edges of something unprecedented, and less than a week into our mission we had lost not just the linguist at the border but our anthropologist and our psychologist.

"Okay, I give up," the surveyor said, throwing down her rifle and sagging into a chair in front of the anthropologist's tent as I rummaged around inside of it. "I'm going to believe you for now. I'm going to believe you because I don't really have a choice. Because I don't have any better theories. What should we do now?"

There still weren't any clues in the anthropologist's tent. The horror of what had happened to her was still hitting me. To be coerced into your own death. If I was right, the psychologist was a murderer, much more so than whatever had killed the anthropologist.

When I didn't answer the surveyor, she repeated herself, with extra emphasis: "So what the hell are we going to do now?"

Emerging from the tent, I said, "We examine the samples I took, we develop the photographs and go through them. Then, tomorrow, we probably go back down into the tower."

The surveyor gave a harsh laugh as she struggled to find words. Her face seemed to almost want to pull apart for a second, perhaps from the strain of fighting off the ghost of some hypnotic suggestion. Finally she got it out: "No. I'm not going back down into that place. And it's a *tunnel*, not a tower."

"What do you want to do instead?" I asked.

As if she'd broken through some barrier, the words now came faster, more determined. "We go back to the border and await extraction. We don't have the resources to continue, and if you're right the psychologist is out there right now plotting something, even if it's just what excuses to give us. And if she's not, if she's dead or injured because something attacked her, that's another reason to get the hell out." She had lit a cigarette, one of the few we'd been given. She blew two long plumes of smoke out of her nose.

"I'm not ready to go back," I told her. "Not yet." I wasn't near ready, despite what had happened.

"You prefer this place, you really do, don't you?" the surveyor said. It wasn't really a question; a kind of pity or disgust infused her voice. "You think this is going to last much longer? Let me tell you, even on military maneuvers designed to simulate negative outcomes, I've seen better odds."

Fear was driving her, even if she was right. I decided to steal my delaying tactics from the psychologist.

"Let's just look at what we brought back, and then we can decide what to do. You can always head back to the border tomorrow."

She took another drag on the cigarette, digesting that. The border was still a four-day hike away.

"True enough," she said, relenting for the moment.

I didn't say what I was thinking: That it might not be that simple. That she might make it back across the border only in the abstract sense that my husband had, stripped of what made her unique. But I didn't want her to feel as if she had no way out.

I spent the rest of the afternoon looking at samples under the microscope, on the makeshift table outside of my tent. The surveyor busied herself with developing the photographs in the tent that doubled as a darkroom, a frustrating process for anyone used to digital uploads. Then, while the photos were resting, she went back through the remnants of maps and documents the prior expedition had left at the base camp.

My samples told a series of cryptic jokes with punch lines I didn't understand. The cells of the biomass that made up the words on the wall had an unusual structure, but they still fell within an acceptable range. Or, those cells were doing a magnificent job of mimicking certain species of saprotrophic organisms. I made a mental note to take a sample of the wall from behind the words. I had no idea how deeply the filaments had taken root, or if there were nodes beneath and those filaments were only sentinels.

The tissue sample from the hand-shaped creature resisted any interpretation, and that was strange but told me nothing. By which I mean I found no cells in the sample, just a solid amber surface with air bubbles in it. At the time, I interpreted this as a contaminated sample or evidence that this organism decomposed quickly. Another thought came to me too late to test: that, having absorbed the organism's spores, I was causing a reaction in the sample. I didn't have the medical facilities to run the kinds of diagnostics that might have revealed any further changes to my body or mind since the encounter.

Then there was the sample from the anthropologist's vial. I had left it for last for the obvious reasons. I had the surveyor take a section, put it on the slide, and write down what she saw through the microscope.

"Why?" she asked. "Why did you need me to do this?"

I hesitated. "Hypothetically . . . there could be contamination."

Such a hard face, jaw tight. "Hypothetically, why would you be any more or less contaminated than me?"

I shrugged. "No particular reason. I was the first one to find the words on the wall, though."

She looked at me as if I had spouted nonsense, laughed harshly. "We're in so much deeper than that. Do you really think those masks we wore are going to keep us safe? From whatever's going on here?" She was wrong—I thought she was wrong—but I didn't correct her. People trivialize or simplify data for so many reasons.

There was nothing else to be said. She went back to her work as I squinted through the microscope at the sample from whatever had killed the anthropologist. At first I didn't know what I was looking at because it was so unexpected. It was brain tissue—and not just any brain tissue. The cells were remarkably human, with some irregularities. My thought at the time was that the sample *had* been corrupted, but if so not by my presence: The surveyor's notes perfectly described what I saw, and when she looked at the sample again later she confirmed its unchanged nature.

I kept squinting through the microscope lens, and raising my head, and squinting again, as if I couldn't see the sample correctly. Then I settled down and stared at it until it became just a series of squiggles and circles. Was it really human? Was it *pretending* to be human? As I said, there were irregularities. And how had the anthropologist taken the sample? Just walked up to the *thing* with an ice-cream scoop and asked, "Can I take a biopsy of your brain?" No, the sample had to come from the margins, from the exterior. Which meant it couldn't be brain tissue, which meant it was definitely not human. I felt unmoored, drifting, once again.

About then, the surveyor strode over and threw the developed photographs down on my table. "Useless," she said.

Every photograph of the words on the wall was a riot of luminous, out-of-focus color. Every photograph of anything other than the words had come out as pure darkness. The few in-between photos were also out of focus. I knew this was probably because of the slow, steady breathing of the walls, which might also have been giving off some kind of heat or other agent of distortion. A thought that made me realize I had not taken a sample of the walls. I had recognized the words were organisms. I had known the walls were, too, but my brain had still registered *walls* as inert, part of a structure. Why sample them?

"I know," the surveyor said, misunderstanding my cursing. "Any luck with the samples?"

"No. No luck at all," I said, still staring at the photographs. "Anything in the maps and papers?"

The surveyor snorted. "Not a damn thing. Nothing. Except they all seem fixated on the lighthouse—watching the lighthouse, going to the lighthouse, living in the goddamn lighthouse."

"So we have nothing."

The surveyor ignored that, said, "What do we do now?" It was clear she hated asking the question.

"Eat dinner," I said. "Take a little stroll along the perimeter to make sure the psychologist isn't hiding in the bushes. Think about what we're doing tomorrow."

"I'll tell you one thing we're not doing tomorrow. We're not going back into the tunnel."

"Tower."

She glared at me.

There was no point in arguing with her.

At dusk, the familiar moaning came to us from across the salt-marsh flats as we ate our dinner around the campfire. I hardly noticed it, intent on my meal. The food tasted so good, and I did not know why. I gobbled it up, had seconds, while the surveyor, baffled, just stared at me. We had little or nothing to say to each other. Talking would have meant planning, and nothing I wanted to plan would please her.

The wind picked up, and it began to rain. I saw each drop fall as a perfect, faceted liquid diamond, refracting light even in the gloom, and I could smell the sea and picture the roiling waves. The wind was like something alive; it entered every pore of me and it, too, had a smell, carrying with it the earthiness of the marsh reeds. I had tried to ignore the change in the confined space of the tower, but my senses still seemed too acute, too sharp. I was adapting to it, but at times like this, I remembered that just a day ago I had been someone else.

We took turns standing watch. Loss of sleep seemed less foolhardy than letting the psychologist sneak up on us unannounced; she knew the location of every perimeter trip wire and we had no time to disarm and reset them. I let the surveyor take the first watch as a gesture of good faith.

In the middle of the night, the surveyor came in to wake me up for the second shift, but I was already awake because of the thunder. Grumpily, she headed off to bed. I doubt she trusted me; I just think she couldn't keep her eyes open a moment longer after the stresses of the day.

The rain renewed its intensity. I didn't worry that we'd be blown away—these tents were army regulation and could withstand anything short of a hurricane—but if I was going to be awake anyway, I wanted to experience the storm. So I walked outside, into the welter of the stinging water, the gusting pockets of wind. I already could hear the surveyor snoring in her tent; she probably had slept through much worse. The dull emergency lights glowed from the edges of the camp, making the tents into triangles of shadow. Even the darkness seemed more alive to me, surrounding me like something physical. I can't even say it was a sinister presence.

I felt in that moment as if it were all a dream—the training, my former life, the world I had left behind. None of that mattered anymore. Only this place mattered, only this moment, and not because the psychologist had hypnotized me. In the grip of that powerful emotion, I stared out toward the coast, through the jagged narrow spaces between the trees. There, a greater darkness gathered, the confluence of the night, the clouds, and the sea. Somewhere beyond, another border.

Then, through that darkness, I saw it: a flicker of orange light. Just a touch of illumination, too far up in the sky. This puzzled me, until I realized it must originate with the lighthouse. As I watched, the flicker moved to the left and up slightly before being snuffed out, then reappeared a few minutes later much higher, then was snuffed out for good. I waited for the light to return, but it never did. For some reason, the longer the light stayed out, the more restless I became, as if in this strange place a light—any sort of light—was a sign of civilization.

There had been a storm that final full day alone with my husband after he returned from the eleventh expedition. A day that had the clarity of dream, of something strange yet familiar—familiar routine but strange calmness, even more than I had become accustomed to before he left.

In those last weeks before the expedition, we had argued—violently. I had shoved him up against a wall, thrown things at him. Anything to break through the armor of resolve that I know now might have been thrust upon him by hypnotic suggestion. "If you go," I had told him, "you might not come back, and you can't be sure I'll be waiting for you if you do." Which had made him laugh, infuriatingly, and say, "Oh, have you been waiting for me all this time? Have I arrived yet?" He was set in his course by then, and any obstruction was a source of rough humor for him—and that would have been entirely natural, hypnosis or not. It was entirely in keeping with his personality to become set on something and follow it, regardless of the consequences. To let an impulse become a compulsion, especially if he thought he was contributing to a cause greater than himself. It was one reason he had stayed in the navy for a second tour.

Our relationship had been thready for a while, in part because he was gregarious and I preferred solitude. This had once been a source of strength in our relationship, but no longer. Not only had I found him handsome but I *admired* his confident, outgoing nature, his need to be around people—I recognized this as a healthy counterbalance to my personality. He had a good sense of humor, too, and when we first met, at a crowded local park, he snuck past my reticence by pretending we were both detectives working a case and were there to watch a suspect. Which led to making up facts about the lives of the busy hive of people buzzing around us, and then about each other.

At first, I must have seemed mysterious to him, my guardedness, my need to be alone, even after he thought he'd gotten inside my defenses. Either I was a puzzle to be solved or he just thought that once he got to know me better, he could still break through to some other place, some core where another person lived inside of me. During one of our fights, he admitted as much—tried to make his "volunteering" for the expedition a sign of how much I had pushed him away, before taking it back later, ashamed. I told him point-blank, so there would be no mistake: This person he wanted to know better did not exist; I was who I seemed to be from the outside. That would never change.

Early in our relationship, I had told my husband about the swimming pool as we lay in bed, something we did a lot of back then. He had been captivated, possibly even thinking there were more interesting revelations to come. He had pushed aside the parts that spoke of an isolated childhood, to focus entirely on the pool itself.

"I would have sailed boats on it."

"Captained by Old Flopper, no doubt," I replied. "And everything would have been happy and wonderful."

"No. Because I would have found you surly and willful and grim. Fairly grim."

"I would have found you frivolous and wished really hard for the turtles to scuttle your boat."

"If they did, I would just have rebuilt it even better and told everyone about the grim kid who talked to frogs."

I had never talked to the frogs; I despised anthropomorphizing animals. "So what has changed if we wouldn't have liked each other as kids?" I asked.

"Oh, I would have liked you despite that," he said, grinning. "You would have fascinated me, and I would have followed you anywhere. Without hesitation."

So we fit back then, in our odd way. We clicked, by being opposites, and took pride in the idea that this made us strong. We reveled in this construct so much, for so long, that it was a wave that did not break until after we were married . . . and then it destroyed us over time, in depressingly familiar ways.

But none of this—the good or the bad—mattered when he returned from the expedition. I asked no questions, did not bring up any of our past arguments. I knew when I woke up beside him that morning after his return that our time together was already running out.

I made him breakfast, while outside the rain beat down, lightning cracking nearby. We sat at the kitchen table, which had a view, through the sliding-glass doors, of the back-yard, and had an excruciatingly polite conversation over eggs and bacon. He admired the gray shape of the new bird feeder I had put in, and the water feature that now rip-pled with raindrops. I asked him if he had gotten enough sleep, and how he felt. I even asked again questions from the night before, like whether the journey back had been tough.

"No," he said, "effortless," flashing an imitation of his old infuriating smile.

"How long did it take?" I asked.

"No time at all." I couldn't read his expression, but in its blankness I sensed something mournful, something left in-side that wanted to communicate but couldn't. My husband had never been mournful or melancholy as long as I had known him, and this frightened me a little.

He asked me how my research was going, and I told him about some of the new developments. At the time, I worked for a company devoted to the creation of natural products that broke down plastics and other nonbiodegradable sub-stances. It was boring. Before that, I had been out in the field, taking advantage of various research grants. Before that, I had been a radical environmentalist, participating in protests and employed by a nonprofit to call potential donors on the phone.

"And your work?" I asked, tentative, not sure how much

more circling I could do, ready at a moment's notice to dart away from the mystery.

"Oh, you know," he said, as if he'd only been away a few weeks, as if I were a colleague, not his lover, his wife. "Oh, you know, the same as always. Nothing really new." He drank deeply from his orange juice—really drank to savor it so that for a minute or two nothing existed in the house but his enjoyment. Then he casually asked about other improvements around the house.

After breakfast, we sat out on the porch, watching the sheets of rain, the puddles collecting in the herb garden. We read for a while, then went back inside and made love. It was a kind of repetitive, trancelike fucking, comfortable only because the weather cocooned us. If I had been pretending up until that point, I couldn't fool myself any longer that my husband was entirely present.

Then it was lunch, and then television—I found a rerun of a two-man sailing race for him—and more banal talk. He asked about some of his friends, but I had no answers. I never saw them. They'd never really been my friends; I didn't cultivate friends, I had just inherited them from my husband.

We tried to play a board game and laughed at some of the sillier questions. Then weird gaps in his knowledge became apparent and we stopped, a kind of silence settling over us. He read the paper and caught up on his favorite magazines, watched the news. Or perhaps he only pretended to do those things.

When the rain stopped, I woke from a brief nap on the couch to find him gone from beside me. I tried not to panic when I checked every room and couldn't find him anywhere. I went outside and eventually found him around the side of the house. He was standing in front of the boat he had bought a few years back, which we could never fit in the garage. It was just a cruiser, about twenty feet long, but he loved it.

As I came and curled my arm around his, he had a puzzled, almost forlorn look on his face, as if he could remember that the boat was important to him but not why. He didn't acknowledge my presence, kept staring at the boat with a growing blank intensity. I could feel him trying to recall something important; I just didn't realize until much later that it had to do with me. That he could have told me something vital, then, there, if he could only have recalled what. So we just stood there, and although I could feel the heat and weight of him beside me, the steady sound of his breathing, we were living apart.

After a while, I couldn't take it—the sheer directionless anonymity of his distress, his silence. I led him back inside. He didn't stop me. He didn't protest. He didn't try to look back over his shoulder at the boat. I think that's when I made my decision. If he had only looked back. If he had just resisted me, even for a moment, it might have been different.

At dinner, as he was finishing, they came for him in four or five unmarked cars and a surveillance van. They did not come in rough or shouting, with handcuffs and weapons on display. Instead, they approached him with respect, one might almost say fear: the kind of watchful gentleness you might display if about to handle an unexploded bomb. He went without protest, and I let them take this stranger from my house.

I couldn't have stopped them, but I also didn't want to.

The last few hours I had coexisted with him in a kind of rising panic, more and more convinced that whatever had happened to him in Area X had turned him into a shell, an automaton going through the motions. Someone I had never known. With every atypical act or word, he was driving me further from the memory of the person I had known, and despite everything that had happened, preserving that idea of him was important. That is why I called the special number he had left me for emergencies: I didn't know what to do with him, couldn't coexist with him any longer in this altered state. Seeing him leave I felt mostly a sense of relief, to be honest, not guilt at betrayal. What else could I have done?

As I have said, I visited him in the observation facility right up until the end. Even under hypnosis in those taped interviews, he had nothing new to say, really, unless it was kept from me. I remember mostly the repetitious sadness in his words. "I am walking forever on the path from the border to base camp. It is taking a long time, and I know it will take even longer to get back. There is no one with me. I am all by myself. The trees are not trees the birds are not birds and I am not me but just something that has been walking for a very long time . . ."

This was really the only thing I discovered in him after his return: a deep and unending solitude, as if he had been granted a gift that he didn't know what to do with. A gift that was poison to him and eventually killed him. But would it have killed me? That was the question that crept into my mind even as I stared into his eyes those last few times, willing myself to know his thoughts and failing.

As I labored at my increasingly repetitive job, in a sterile lab, I kept thinking about Area X, and how I would never know what it was like without going there. No one could really tell me, and no account could possibly be a substitute. So several months after my husband died, I volunteered for an Area X expedition. A spouse of a former expedition member had never signed up before. I think they accepted me in part because they wanted to see if that connection might make a difference. I think they accepted me as an experiment. But then again, maybe from the start they expected me to sign up.

By morning, it had stopped raining and the sky was a searing blue, almost devoid of clouds. Only the pine needles strewn across the top of our tents and the dirty puddles and fallen tree limbs on the ground told of the storm the night before. The brightness infecting my senses had spread to my chest; I can describe it no other way. Internally, there was a *brightness* in me, a kind of prickling energy and anticipation that pushed hard against my lack of sleep. Was this part of the change? But even so, it didn't matter—I had no way to combat what might be happening to me.

I also had a decision to make, finding myself torn between the lighthouse and the tower. Some part of the brightness wanted to return to darkness at once, and the logic of this related to nerve, or lack of it. To plunge right back into the tower, without thought, without planning, would be an act of faith, of sheer resolve or recklessness with nothing else behind it. But now I also knew that *someone* had been in the lighthouse the night before. If the psychologist had sought refuge there, and I could track her down, then I might gain more insight into the tower before exploring it further. This seemed of increasing importance, more so than the night before, because the number of unknowns the tower represented had multiplied tenfold. So by the time I talked to the surveyor, I had decided on the lighthouse.

The morning had the scent and feel of a fresh start, but it was not to be. If the surveyor had wanted no part of a return to the tower, then she equally had no interest in the lighthouse.

"You don't want to find out if the psychologist is there?"

The surveyor gave me a look as if I had said something idiotic. "Holed up in a high position with clear lines of sight in every direction? In a place they've told us has a weapons cache? I'll take my chances here. If you were smart, you'd do the same. You might 'find out' that you don't like a bullet hole in the head. Besides, she might be somewhere else."

Her stubbornness tore at me. I didn't want to split up for purely practical reasons—it was true we had been told prior expeditions had stored weapons at the lighthouse—and because I believed it more likely that the surveyor would try to go home without me there.

"It's the lighthouse or the tower," I said, trying to sidestep the issue. "And it would be better for us if we found the psychologist before we went back down into the tower. She saw whatever killed the anthropologist. She knows more than she's told us." The unspoken thought: That perhaps if a day passed, or two, whatever lived in the tower, slowly making words on the wall, would have disappeared or gotten so far ahead of us we would never catch up. But that brought to mind a disturbing image of the tower as endless, with infinite levels descending into the earth.

The surveyor folded her arms. "You really don't get it, do you? This mission is over."

Was she afraid? Did she just not like me enough to say yes? Whatever the reason, her opposition angered me, as did the smug look on her face.

In the moment, I did something that I regret now. I said, "There's no *reward in the risk* of going back to the tower right now."

I thought I had been subtle in my intonation of one of the psychologist's hypnotic cues, but a shudder passed over the surveyor's face, a kind of temporary disorientation. When it cleared, the look that remained told me she understood what I had tried to do. It wasn't even a look of surprise; more that in her mind I had confirmed an impression of me that had been slowly forming but was now set. Now, too, I had learned that hypnotic cues only worked for the psychologist.

"You'd do anything, wouldn't you, to get your way," the surveyor said, but the fact was: She held the rifle. What weapon did I really have? And I told myself it was because I didn't want the anthropologist's death to be meaningless that I had suggested this course of action.

When I did not reply, she sighed, then said, with weariness in her voice, "You know, I finally figured it out while I was developing those useless photographs. What bothered me the most. It's not the thing in the tunnel or the way you conduct yourself or anything the psychologist did. It's this rifle I'm holding. This damn rifle. I stripped it down to clean it and found it was made of thirty-year-old parts, cobbled together. *Nothing* we brought with us is from the present. Not our clothes, not our shoes. It's all old junk. Restored crap. We've been living in the past this whole time. In some sort of *reenactment*. And why?" She made a derisive sound. "You don't even know why."

It was as much as she'd ever said to me at one time. I wanted to say that this information registered as little more than the mildest of surprises in the hierarchy of what we had thus far discovered. But I didn't. All I had left was to be succinct.

"Will you remain here until I return?" I asked.

This was now the essential question, and I didn't like the speed of her reply, or its tone.

"Whatever you want."

"Don't say anything you can't back up," I said. I had long ago stopped believing in promises. Biological imperatives, yes. Environmental factors, yes. Promises, no.

"Fuck off," she said.

So that's how we left it—her leaning back in that rickety chair, holding her assault rifle, as I went off to discover the source of the light I had seen the night before. I had with me a knapsack full of food and water, along with two of the guns, equipment to take samples, and one of the microscopes. Somehow I felt safer taking a microscope with me. Some part of me, too, no matter how I had tried to convince the surveyor to come with me, welcomed the chance to explore alone, to not be dependent on, or worried about, anyone else.

I looked back a couple of times before the trail twisted away, and the surveyor was still sitting there, staring at me like a distorted reflection of who I'd been just days before.

03: **IMMOLATION**

Now a strange mood took hold of me, as I walked silent and alone through the last of the pines and the cypress knees that seemed to float in the black water, the gray moss that coated everything. It was as if I traveled through the landscape with the sound of an expressive and intense aria playing in my ears. Everything was imbued with emotion, awash in it, and I was no longer a biologist but somehow the crest of a wave building and building but never crashing to shore. I saw with such new eyes the subtleties of the transition to the marsh, the salt flats. As the trail became a raised berm, dull, algae-choked lakes spread out to the right and a canal flanked it to the left. Rough channels of water meandered out in a maze through a forest of reeds on the canal side, and islands, oases of wind-contorted trees, appeared in the distance like sudden revelations. The stooped and blackened appearance of these trees was shocking against the vast and shimmering gold-brown of the reeds. The strange quality of the light upon this habitat, the stillness of it all, the sense of *waiting*, brought me halfway to a kind of ecstasy.

Beyond, the lighthouse stood, and before that, I knew, the remains of a village, also marked on the map. But in front of me was the trail, strewn at times with oddly tortured-looking pieces of heavy white driftwood flung far inland from past hurricanes. Tiny red grasshoppers inhabited the long grass in legions, with only a few frogs present to feast on them, and flattened grass tunnels marked where the huge reptiles had, after bathing in the sun, slid back into the water. Above, raptors searched the ground below for prey, circling as if in geometric patterns so controlled was their flight.

In that cocoon of timelessness, with the lighthouse seeming to remain distant no matter how long I walked, I had more time to think about the tower and our expedition. I felt that I had abdicated my responsibility to that point, which was to consider those elements found inside of the tower as part of a vast biological entity that might or might not be terrestrial. But contemplating the sheer enormity of that idea on a macro level would have broken my mood like an avalanche crashing into my body.

So . . . what did I know? What were the specific details? An . . . organism . . . was writing living words along the interior walls of the tower, and may have been doing so for a very long time. Whole ecosystems had been born and now flourished among the words, dependent on them, before dying off as the words faded. But this was a side effect of creating the right conditions, a viable habitat. It was important only in that the adaptations of the creatures living in the words could tell me something about the tower. For example, the spores I had inhaled, which pointed to a *truthful seeing*.

I was brought up short by this idea, the wind-lashed marsh reeds a wide, blurred ripple all around me. I had assumed the psychologist had hypnotized me into seeing the tower as a physical construction not a biological entity, and that an effect of the spores had made me resistant to this hypnotic suggestion. But what if the process had been more complex? What if, by whatever means, the *tower* emanated an effect, too—one that constituted a kind of defensive mimicry, and the spores had made me immune to that illusion?

Telescoping out from this context, I had several questions and few answers. What role did the *Crawler* serve? (I had decided it was important to assign a name to the maker-of-words.) What was the purpose of the physical "recitation" of the words? Did the actual words matter, or would any words do? Where had the words come from? What was the interplay between the words and the tower-creature? Put another way: Were the words a form of symbiotic or parasitic communication between the Crawler and the Tower? Either the Crawler was an *emissary* of the Tower or had originally existed independent from it and come into its orbit later. But without the damned missing sample of the Tower wall, I couldn't really begin to guess.

Which brought me back to the words. *Where lies the strangling fruit that came from the hand of the sinner . . .* Wasps and birds and other nest-builders often used some core, irreplaceable substance or material to create their structures but would also incorporate whatever they could find in their immediate environment. This might explain the seemingly random nature of the words. It was just building material, and perhaps this explained why our superiors had forbidden high-tech being brought into Area X, because they knew it could be used in unknown and powerful ways by whatever occupied this place.

Several new ideas detonated inside me as I watched a marsh hawk dive into the reeds and come up with a rabbit struggling in its talons. First, that the words—the line of them, their physicality—were absolutely essential to the well-being of either the Tower or the Crawler, or both. I had seen the faint skeletons of so many past lines of writing that one might assume some biological imperative for the Crawler's work. This process might feed into the reproductive cycle of the Tower or the Crawler. Perhaps the Crawler depended upon it, and it had some subsidiary benefit to the Tower. Or vice versa. Perhaps words didn't matter because it was a process of *fertilization*, only completed when the entire left-hand wall of the Tower had a line of words running along its length.

Despite my attempt to sustain the aria in my head, I experienced a jarring return to reality as I worked through these possibilities. Suddenly I was just a person trudging across a natural landscape of a type I had seen before. There were too many variables, not enough data, and I was making some base assumptions that might not be true. For one thing, in all of this I assumed that neither Crawler nor Tower was intelligent, in the sense of *possessing free will*. My procreation theory would still apply in such a widening context, but there were other possibilities. The role of ritual, for example, in certain cultures and societies. How I longed for access to the anthropologist's mind now, even though in studying social insects I had gained some insight into the same areas of scientific endeavor.

And if not ritual, I was back to the purposes of communication, this time in a conscious sense, not a biological one.

What could the words on the wall communicate to the Tower? I had to assume, or thought I did, that the Crawler didn't just live in the Tower—it went far afield to gather the words, and it had to assimilate them, even if it didn't understand them, before it came back to the Tower. The Crawler had to in a sense *memorize* them, which was a form of absorption. The strings of sentences on the Tower's walls could be *evidence* brought back by the Crawler to be analyzed by the Tower.

But there is a limit to thinking about even a small piece of something monumental. You still see the shadow of the whole rearing up behind you, and you become lost in your thoughts in part from the panic of realizing the *size* of that imagined leviathan. I had to leave it there, compartmentalized, until I could write it all down, and seeing it on the page, begin to divine the true meaning. And now the lighthouse had finally gotten larger on the horizon. This presence weighed on me as I realized that the surveyor had been correct about at least one thing. Anyone within the lighthouse would see me coming for miles. Then, too, that other effect of the spores, the brightness in my chest, continued to sculpt me as I walked, and by the time I reached the deserted village that told me I was halfway to the lighthouse, I believed I could have run a marathon. I did not trust that feeling. I felt, in so many ways, that I was being lied to.

Having seen the preternatural calm of the members of the eleventh expedition, I had often thought during our training of the benign reporting from the first expedition. Area X, before the ill-defined Event that locked it behind the border thirty years ago and made it subject to so many inexplicable occurrences, had been part of a wilderness that lay adjacent to a military base. People had still lived there, on what amounted to a wildlife refuge, but not many, and they tended to be the tight-lipped descendants of fisherfolk. Their disappearance might have seemed to some a simple intensifying of a process begun generations before.

When Area X first appeared, there was vagueness and confusion, and it is still true that out in the world not many people know that it exists. The government's version of events emphasized a localized environmental catastrophe stemming from experimental military research. This story leaked into the public sphere over a period of several months so that, like the proverbial frog in a hot pot, people found the news entering their consciousness gradually as part of the general daily noise of media oversaturation about ongoing ecological devastation. Within a year or two, it had become the province of conspiracy theorists and other fringe elements. By the time I volunteered and was given the security clearance to have a firm picture of the truth, the idea of an "Area X" lingered in many people's minds like a dark fairy tale, something they did not want to think about too closely. If they thought about it at all. We had so many other problems.

During training, we were told that the first expedition went in two years after the Event, after scientists found a way to breach the border. It was the first expedition that set up the base-camp perimeter and provided a rough map of Area X, confirming many of the landmarks. They discovered a pristine wilderness devoid of any human life. They found what some might call a preternatural silence.

"I felt as if I were both freer than ever before and more constrained," one member of the expedition said. "I felt as if I could do anything *as long as I did not mind being watched*."

Others mentioned feelings of euphoria and extremes of sexual desire, for which there was no explanation and which, ultimately, their superiors found unimportant.

If one could spot anomalies in their reports, these anomalies lay at the fringes. For one thing, we never saw their journals; instead, they offered up their accounts in long recorded interviews. This, to me, hinted at some avoidance of their direct experience, although at the time I also thought perhaps I was being paranoid, in a nonclinical sense.

Some of them offered descriptions of the abandoned village that seemed inconsistent to me. The warping and level of ruination depicted a place abandoned for much longer than a few years. But if someone had caught this strangeness earlier, any such observation had been stricken from the record.

I am convinced now that I and the rest of the expedition were given access to these records for the simple reason that, for certain kinds of classified information, it did not matter what we knew or didn't know. There was only one logical conclusion: Experience told our superiors that few if any of us would be coming back.

The deserted village had so sunk into the natural landscape of the coast that I did not see it until I was upon it. The trail dipped into a depression of sorts, and there lay the village, fringed by more stunted trees. Only a few roofs remained on the twelve or thirteen houses, and the trail through had crumbled into porous rubble. Some outer walls still stood, dark rotting wood splotched with lichen, but for the most part these walls had fallen away and left me with a peculiar glimpse of the interiors: the remains of chairs and tables, a child's toys, rotted clothing, ceiling beams brought to earth, covered in moss and vines. There was a sharp smell of chemicals in that place, and more than one dead animal, decomposing into the mulch. Some of the houses had, over time, slid into the canal to the left and looked in their skeletal remains like creatures struggling to leave the water. It all seemed like something that had happened a century ago, and what was left were just vague recollections of the event.

But in what had been kitchens or living rooms or bedrooms, I also saw a few peculiar eruptions of moss or lichen, rising four, five, feet tall, misshapen, the vegetative matter forming an approximation of limbs and heads and torsos. As if there had been runoff from the material, too heavy for gravity, that had congregated at the foot of these objects. Or perhaps I imagined this effect.

One particular tableau struck me in an almost emotional way. Four such eruptions, one "standing" and three decomposed to the point of "sitting" in what once must have been a living room with a coffee table and a couch—all facing some point at the far end of the room where lay only the crumbling soft brick remains of a fireplace and chimney. The smell of lime and mint unexpectedly arose, cutting through the must, the loam.

I did not want to speculate on that tableau, its meaning, or what element of the past it represented. No sense of peace emanated from that place, only a feeling of something left unresolved or still in progress. I wanted to move on, but first I took samples. I had a need to document what I had found, and a photograph didn't seem sufficient, given how the others had turned out. I cut a piece of the moss from the "forehead" of one of the eruptions. I took splinters of the wood. I even scraped the flesh of the dead animals—a stricken fox, curled up and dry, along with a kind of rat that must have died only a day or two before.

It was just after I had left the village that a peculiar thing happened. I was startled to see a sudden double line coming down the canal toward me, cutting through the water. My binoculars were no use as the water was opaque from the glare of the sun. Otters? Fish? Something else? I pulled out my gun.

Then the dolphins breached, and it was almost as vivid a dislocation as that first descent into the Tower. I knew that the dolphins here sometimes ventured in from the sea, had adapted to the freshwater. But when the mind expects a certain range of possibilities, any explanation that falls outside of that expectation can surprise. Then something more wrenching occurred. As they slid by, the nearest one rolled slightly to the side, and it stared at me with an eye that did not, in that brief flash, resemble a dolphin eye to me. It was painfully human, almost familiar. In an instant that glimpse was gone and they had submerged again, and I had no way to verify what I had seen. I stood there, watched those twinned lines disappear up the canal, back toward the deserted village. I had the unsettling thought that the natural world around me had become a kind of camouflage.

A little shaken, I continued toward the lighthouse, which now loomed larger, almost heavy, its black-and-white stripes topped with red making it somehow authoritarian. I would have no further shelter before I reached my destination. I would stand out to whoever or whatever watched from that vantage as something unnatural in that landscape, something that was foreign. Perhaps even a threat.

It was almost noon by the time I reached the lighthouse. I had been careful to drink water and have a snack on my journey, but I still arrived weary; perhaps the lack of sleep had caught up with me. But then, too, the last three hundred yards to reach the lighthouse were tension-filled, as I kept remembering the surveyor's warning. I had a gun out, held down by my side, for all the good it would do against a high-powered rifle. I kept looking at the little window halfway up its swirled black-and-white surface, and then to the large panoramic windows at the top, alert for any movement.

The lighthouse was positioned just before a natural crest of the dunes that resembled a curled wave facing the ocean, the beach spread out beyond. Up close it gave the strong appearance of having been converted into a fortress, a fact conveniently left out of our training. This only confirmed the impression I had formed from farther out, because although the grass was still long, no trees at all grew along the trail from about a quarter mile out; I had found only old stumps. When within an eighth mile, I had taken a look with my binoculars and noticed an approximately ten-foot circular wall rising from the landward side of the lighthouse that had clearly not been part of the original construction.

On the seaward side, another wall, an even stouter-looking fortification high on the crumbling dune, topped with broken glass and, as I drew near, I could see crenellations that created lines of sight for rifles. It was all in danger of falling down the slope onto the beach below. But for it not to have done so already, whoever had built it must have dug its foundations deep. It appeared that some past defenders of the lighthouse had been at war with the sea. I did not like this wall because it provided evidence of a very specific kind of insanity.

At some point, too, someone had taken the time and effort to rappel down the sides of the lighthouse and attach jagged shards of glass with some strong glue or other adhesive. These glass daggers started about one-third of the way up and continued to the penultimate level, just below the glass-enclosed beacon. At that point, a kind of metal collar extended out a good two or three feet, and this defensive element had been enhanced with rusty barbed wire.

Someone had tried very hard to keep others out. I thought of the Crawler and the words on the wall. I thought of the fixation with the lighthouse in the fragments of notes left by the last expedition. But despite these discordant elements, I was glad to reach the shadow of that cool, dank wall around the landward side of the lighthouse. From that angle, no one could shoot at me from the top, or the window in the middle. I had passed through the first gauntlet. If the psychologist was inside, she had decided against violence for now.

The defensive wall on the landward side had reached a level of disrepair that reflected years of neglect. A large, irregular hole led to the lighthouse's front door. That door had exploded inward and only fragments of wood clung to the rusted hinges. A purple flowering vine had colonized the lighthouse wall and curled itself around the remains of the door on its left side. There was comfort in that, for whatever had happened with such violence must have occurred long ago.

The darkness beyond, however, made me wary. I knew from the floor plan I had seen during training that this bottom level of the lighthouse had three outer rooms, with the stairs leading to the top somewhere to the left, and that to the right the rooms opened up into a back area with at least one more larger space. Plenty of places for someone to hide.

I picked up a stone and half threw, half rolled it onto the floor beyond those crushed double doors. It clacked and spun across tile and disappeared from view. I heard no other sound, no movement, no suggestion of breathing beyond my own. Gun still drawn, I entered as quietly as I was able, sliding with my shoulder along the left-hand wall, searching for the entry point to the stairs leading upward.

The outer rooms at the base of the lighthouse were empty. The sound of the wind was muffled, the walls thick, and only two small windows toward the front brought any light inside; I had to use my flashlight. As my eyes adjusted, the sense of devastation, of loneliness, grew and grew. The purple flowering vine ended just inside, unable to thrive in the darkness. There were no chairs. The tiles of the floor were covered in dirt and debris. No personal effects remained in those outer rooms. In the middle of a wide open space, I found the stairs. No one stood on those steps to watch me, but I had the impression someone could have been there a moment before. I thought about climbing to the top first rather than exploring the back rooms, but then decided against it. Better to think like the surveyor, with her military training, and clear the area now, even though someone could always come in the front door while I was up there.

The back room told a different story than the front rooms did. My imagination could only reconstruct what might have happened in the broadest, crudest terms. Here stout oak tables had been overturned to form crude defensive barricades. Some of the tables were full of bullet holes and others appeared half-melted or shredded by gunfire. Beyond the remains of the tables, the dark splotches across the walls and pooled on the floor told of unspeakable and sudden violence. Dust had settled over everything, along with the cool, flat smell of slow decay, and I could see rat droppings and signs of a cot or a bed having been placed in a corner at some later date . . . although who could have slept among such reminders of a massacre? Someone, too, had carved their initials into one of the tables: "R.S. was here." The marks looked fresher than the rest of it. Maybe you carved your initials when visiting a war monument, if you were insensitive. Here it stank of bravado to drown out fear.

The stairs awaited, and to quell my rising nausea, I headed back to them and began to climb. I had put my gun away by then, since I needed that hand for balance, but I wished I had the surveyor's assault rifle. I would have felt safer.

It was a strange ascent, in contrast to my descents into the Tower. The brackish quality of the light against those graying interior walls was better than the phosphorescence of the Tower, but what I found on these walls unnerved me just as much, if in a different way. More bloodstains, mostly thick smudges as if several people had bled out while trying to escape attackers from below. Sometimes dribbles of blood. Sometimes a spray.

Words had been written on these walls, but nothing like the words in the Tower. More initials, but also little obscene pictures and a few phrases of a more personal nature. Some longer hints of what might have transpired: "4 boxes of food-stuffs 3 boxes of medical supplies and drinking water for 5 days if rationed; enough bullets for all of us if necessary." Confessions, too, which I won't document here but that had the sincerity and weight of having been written immediately before, or during, moments when the individuals must have thought death was upon them. So many needing so much to communicate what amounted to so little.

Things found on the stairs . . . a discarded shoe . . . a magazine from an automatic pistol . . . a few moldy vials of samples long rotted or turned to rancid liquid . . . a crucifix that looked like it had been dislodged from the wall . . . a clipboard, the wooden part soggy and the metal part deep orange-red from rust . . . and, worst of all, a dilapidated toy rabbit with ragged ears. Perhaps a good-luck symbol smuggled in on an expedition. There had been no children in Area X since the border had come down, as far as I knew.

At roughly the halfway point, I came to a landing, which must have been where I had first seen the flicker of light the night before. The silence still dominated, and I had heard no hint of movement above me. The light was better because of the windows to left and right. Here the blood spatter abruptly cut off, although bullet holes riddled the walls. Bullet casings littered the floor, but someone had taken the time to sweep them off to the sides, leaving the path to the stairs above clear. To the left lay a stack of guns and rifles, some of them ancient, some of them not army-issue. It was hard to tell if anyone had been at them recently. Thinking about what the surveyor had said, I wondered when I would encounter a blunderbuss or some other terrible joke.

Otherwise, there was just the dust and the mold, and a tiny square window looking down on the beach and the reeds. Opposite it, a faded photograph in a broken frame, dangling from a nail. The smudged glass was cracked and half-covered in specks of green mold. The black-and-white photograph showed two men standing at the base of the lighthouse, with a girl off to the side. A circle had been drawn with a marker around one of the men. He looked about fifty years old and wore a fisherman's cap. A sharp eagle's eye gleamed out from a heavy face, the left eye lost to his squint. A thick beard hid all but a hint of a firm chin under it. He didn't smile, but he didn't frown, either. I'd had experience enough with lighthouse keepers to know one when I saw one. But there was also some quality to him, perhaps just because of the strange way the dust framed his face, that made me think of him as the lighthouse keeper. Or perhaps I'd already spent too much time in that place, and my mind was seeking any answer, even to simple questions.

The rounded bulk of the lighthouse behind the three was bright and sharp, the door on the far right in good repair. Nothing like what I had encountered, and I wondered when the photo had been taken. How many years between the photograph and the start of it all. How many years had the lighthouse keeper kept to his schedule and his rituals, lived in that community, gone to the local bar or pub. Perhaps he'd had a wife. Perhaps the girl in the photo was his daughter. Perhaps he'd been a popular man. Or solitary. Or a little of both. Regardless, none of it had mattered in the end.

I stared at him from across the years, trying to tell from the moldy photograph, from the line of his jaw and the reflection of light in his eyes, how he might have reacted, what his last hours might have been like. Perhaps he'd left in time, but probably not. Perhaps he was even moldering on the ground floor in a forgotten corner. Or, and I experienced a sudden shudder, maybe he was waiting for me above, at the top. In some form. I took the photograph out of its frame, shoved it in my pocket. The lighthouse keeper would come with me, although he hardly counted as a good-luck charm. As I left the landing, I had the peculiar thought that I was not the first to pocket the photo, that someone would always come behind to replace it, to circle the lighthouse keeper again.

I continued to encounter additional signs of violence the higher I went, but no more bodies. The closer I came to the top, the more I began to have the sense that someone had lived here recently. The mustiness gave way to the scent of sweat, but also a smell like soap. The stairs had less debris on them, and the walls were clean. By the time I was bending over the last narrow stretch of steps out into the lantern room, the ceiling grown suddenly close, I was sure I would emerge to find someone staring at me.

So I took out my gun again. But, again, no one was there— just a few chairs, a rickety table with a rug beneath it, and the surprise that the thick glass here was still intact. The beacon glass itself lay dull and dormant in the center of the room. You could see for miles to all sides. I stood there for a moment, looking back the way I had come: at the trail that had brought me, at the shadow in the distance that might have been the village, and then to the right, across the last of the marsh, the transition to scrubland and the gnarled bushes punished by the wind off the sea. They, clinging to the soil, stopped it from eroding and helped bulwark the dunes and the sea oats that came next. It was a gentle slope from there to the glittering beach, the surf, and the waves.

A second look, and from the direction of base camp amid the swamp and far distant pines, I could see strands of black smoke, which could have meant anything. But I also could see, from the location of the Tower, a kind of brightness of its own, a sort of refracted phosphorescence, that did not bear thinking about. That I could see it, that I had an affinity to it, agitated me. I was certain no one else left here, not the surveyor, not the psychologist, could see that stirring of the inexplicable.

I turned my attention to the chairs, the table, searching for whatever might give me insight into . . . anything. After about five minutes, I thought to pull back the rug. A square trapdoor measuring about four feet per side lay hidden there. The latch was set into the wood of the floor. I pushed the table out of the way with a terrible rending sound that made me grit my teeth. Then, swiftly, in case someone waited down there, I threw open the trapdoor, shouting out something inane like "I've got a gun!" aiming my weapon with one hand and my flashlight with the other.

I had the distant sense of the weight of my gun dropping to the floor, my flashlight shaking in my hand, though somehow I held on to it. I could not believe what I was staring down at, and I felt lost. The trapdoor opened onto a space about fifteen feet deep and thirty feet wide. The psychologist had clearly been here, for her knapsack, several weapons, bottles of water, and a large flashlight lay off to the left side. But of the psychologist herself there was no sign.

No, what had me gasping for breath, what felt like a punch in the stomach as I dropped to my knees, was the huge mound that dominated the space, a kind of insane midden. I was looking at a pile of papers with hundreds of journals on top of it—just like the ones we had been issued to record our observations of Area X. Each with a job title written on the front. Each, as it turned out, filled with writing. Many, many more than could possibly have been filed by only twelve expeditions.

Can you really imagine what it was like in those first moments, peering down into that dark space, and *seeing that*? Perhaps you can. Perhaps you're staring at it now.

My third and best field assignment out of college required that I travel to a remote location on the western coast, to a curled hook of land at the farthest extremity from civilization, in an area that teetered between temperate and arctic climates. Here the earth had disgorged huge rock formations and old-growth rain forest had sprouted up around them. This world was always moist, the annual rainfall more than seventy inches a year, and not seeing droplets of water on leaves was an extraordinary event. The air was so amazingly clean and the vegetation so dense, so richly green, that every spiral of fern seemed designed to make me feel at peace with the world. Bears and panthers and elk lived in those forests, along with a multitude of bird species. The fish in the streams were mercury-free and enormous.

I lived in a village of about three hundred souls near the coast. I had rented a cottage next to a house at the top of a hill that had belonged to five generations of fisherfolk. A husband and wife, childless, owned the property, and they had the kind of severely laconic quality common to the area. I made no friends there, and I wasn't sure that even long-standing neighbors were friends, either. Only in the local pub that everyone frequented, after a few pints, would you see signs of friendliness and camaraderie. But violence lived in the pub, too, and I kept away most of the time. I was four years away from meeting my future husband, and at the time I wasn't looking for much of anything from anyone.

I had plenty to keep me busy. Every day I drove the hellish winding road, rutted and treacherous even when dry, that led me to the place they called simply Rock Bay. There, sheets of magma that lay beyond the rough beaches had been worn smooth over millions of years and become pitted with tidal pools. At low tide in the morning, I would photograph those tidal pools, take measurements, and catalogue the life found within them, sometimes staying through part of high tide, wading in my rubber boots, the spray from the waves that smashed over the lip of the ledge drenching me.

A species of mussels found nowhere else lived in those tidal pools, in a symbiotic relationship with a fish called a gartner, after its discoverer. Several species of marine snails and sea anemones lurked there, too, and a tough little squid I nicknamed Saint Pugnacious, eschewing its scientific name, because the danger music of its white-flashing luminescence made its mantle look like a pope's hat.

I could easily lose hours there, observing the hidden life of tidal pools, and sometimes I marveled at the fact that I had been given such a gift: not just to lose myself in the present moment so utterly but also to have such solitude, which was all I had ever craved during my studies, my practice to reach this point.

Even then, though, during the drives back, I was grieving the anticipated end of this happiness. Because I knew it had to end eventually. The research grant was only for two years, and who really would care about mussels longer than that, and it's true my research methods could be eccentric. These were the kinds of thoughts I'd have as the expiration date came nearer and the prospects looked dimmer and dimmer for renewal. Against my better judgment, I began to spend more and more time in the pub. I'd wake in the morning, my head fuzzy, sometimes with someone I knew but who was a stranger just leaving, and realize I was one day closer to the end of it all. Running through it, too, was a sense of relief, not as strong as the sadness, but the thought, counter to everything else I felt, that this way I would not become that person the locals saw out on the rocks and still thought of as an outsider. *Oh, that's just the old biologist. She's been here for ages, going crazy studying those mussels. She talks to herself, mutters to herself at the bar, and if you say a kind word . . .*

When I saw those hundreds of journals, I felt for a long moment that I had become that old biologist after all. That's how the madness of the world tries to colonize you: from the outside in, forcing you to live in its reality.

Reality encroaches in other ways, too. At some point during our relationship, my husband began to call me the ghost bird, which was his way of teasing me for not being present enough in his life. It would be said with a kind of creasing at the corner of his lips that almost formed a thin smile, but in his eyes I could see the reproach. If we went to bars with his friends, one of his favorite things to do, I would volunteer only what a prisoner might during an interrogation. They weren't *my* friends, not really, but also I wasn't in the habit of engaging in small talk, nor in broad talk, as I liked to call it. I didn't care about politics except in how politics impinged upon the environment. I wasn't religious. All of my hobbies were bound up in my work. I lived for the work, and I thrilled with the power of that focus but it was also deeply personal. I didn't like to talk about my research. I didn't wear makeup or care about new shoes or the latest music. I'm sure my husband's friends found me taciturn, or worse. Perhaps they even found me unsophisticated, or "strangely uneducated" as I heard one of them say, although I don't know if he was referring to me.

I enjoyed the bars, but not for the same reasons as my husband. I loved the late-night slow burn of *being out*, my mind turning over some problem, some piece of data, while able to appear sociable but still existing apart. He worried too much about me, though, and my need for solitude ate into his enjoyment of talking to friends, who were mostly from the hospital. I would see him trail off in mid-sentence, gazing at me for some sign of my own contentment, as, off to the side, I drank my whiskey neat. "Ghost bird," he would say later, "did you have fun?" I'd nod and smile.

But fun for me was sneaking off to peer into a tidal pool, to grasp the intricacies of the creatures that lived there. Sustenance for me was tied to ecosystem and habitat, orgasm the sudden realization of the interconnectivity of living things. Observation had always meant more to me than interaction. He knew all of this, I think. But I never could express myself that well to him, although I did try, and he did listen. And yet, I was *nothing but* expression in other ways. My sole gift or talent, I believe now, was that places could impress themselves upon me, and I could become a part of them with ease. Even a bar was a type of ecosystem, if a crude one, and to someone entering, someone without my husband's agenda, that person could have seen me sitting there and had no trouble imagining that I was happy in my little bubble of silence. Would have had no trouble believing I fit in.

Yet even as my husband wanted me to be assimilated in a sense, the irony was that *he* wanted to stand out. Seeing that huge pile of journals, this was another thing I thought of: That he had been wrong for the eleventh expedition because of this quality. That here were the indiscriminate accounts of so many souls, and that his account *couldn't possibly stand out*. That, in the end, he'd been reduced to a state that approximated my own.

Those journals, flimsy gravestones, confronted me with my husband's death all over again. I dreaded finding his, dreaded knowing his true account, not the featureless, generic mutterings he had given to our superiors upon his return.

"Ghost bird, do you love me?" he whispered once in the dark, before he left for his expedition training, even though he was the ghost. "Ghost bird, do you need me?" I loved him, but I didn't need him, and I thought that was the way it was supposed to be. A ghost bird might be a hawk in one place, a crow in another, depending on the context. The sparrow that shot up into the blue sky one morning might transform mid-flight into an osprey the next. This was the way of things here. There were no reasons so mighty that they could override the desire to be in accord with the tides and the passage of seasons and the rhythms underlying everything around me.

The journals and other materials formed a moldering pile about twelve feet high and sixteen feet wide that in places near the bottom had clearly turned to compost, the paper rotting away. Beetles and silverfish tended to those archives, and tiny black cockroaches with always moving antennae. Toward the base, and spilling out at the edges, I saw the remains of photographs and dozens of ruined cassette tapes mixed in with the mulch of pages. There, too, I saw evidence of rats. I would have to lower myself down into the midden by means of the ladder nailed to the lip of the trapdoor and trudge through a collapsing garbage hill of disintegrating pulp to uncover anything at all. The scene obliquely embodied the scrap of writing I had encountered on the Tower wall: . . . *the seeds of the dead to share with the worms that gather in the darkness and surround the world with the power of their lives* . . .

I overturned the table and laid it across the narrow entrance to the stairwell. I had no idea where the psychologist had gotten to, but I didn't want her or anyone else surprising me. If someone tried to move the table from below, I would hear it and have time to climb up to greet them with my gun. I also had a sensation I can in hindsight attribute to the brightness growing within me: of a *presence* pressing up from below, impinging on the edges of my senses. A prickling crept across my skin at unexpected times, for no good reason.

I didn't like that the psychologist had stashed all of her gear down with the journals, including what appeared to be most or all of her weapons. For the moment, though, I had to put the puzzle of that out of my mind, along with the still-reverberating tremors from the certain knowledge that most of the training the Southern Reach had given us had been based on a lie. As I lowered myself into that cool, dark, sheltered space beneath, I felt the pull of the brightness within me even more acutely. That was harder to ignore, since I didn't know what it meant.

My flashlight, along with the natural light from the open trapdoor, revealed that the walls of the room were rife with striations of mold, some of which formed dull stripes of red and green. From below, the way the midden spilled out in ripples and hillocks of paper became more apparent. Torn pages, crushed pages, journal covers warped and damp. Slowly the history of exploring Area X could be said to be turning into Area X.

I picked around the edges at first, chose journals at random. Most, at a glance, depicted quite ordinary events, such as those described by the first expedition . . . which could not have been the first expedition. Some were extraordinary only because the dates did not make sense. How many expeditions had really come across the border? Just how much information had been doctored and suppressed, and for how long? Did "twelve" expeditions refer only to the latest iteration of a longer effort, the omission of the rest necessary to quell the doubts of those approached to be volunteers?

What I would call pre-expedition accounts, documented in a variety of forms, also existed in that place. This was the underlying archive of audiocassettes, chewed-at photographs, and decomposing folders full of papers that I had first glimpsed from above—all of it oppressed by the weight of the journals on top. All of it suffused by a dull, damp smell that contained within it a masked sharp stench of decay, which revealed itself in some places and not others. A bewildering confusion of typewritten, printed, and handwritten words piled up in my head alongside half-seen images like a mental facsimile of the midden itself. The clutter at times brought me close to becoming frozen, even without factoring in the contradictions. I became aware of the weight of the photograph in my pocket.

I made some initial rules, as if that would help. I ignored journals that appeared to be written in a shorthand and did not try to decipher those that appeared to be in code. I also started out reading some journals straight through and then decided to force myself to skim. But sampling was sometimes worse. I came across pages that described unspeakable acts that I still cannot bring myself to set down in words. Entries that mentioned periods of "remission" and "cessation" followed by "flare-ups" and "horrible manifestations." No matter how long Area X had existed, and how many expeditions had come here, I could tell from these accounts that for years before there had ever been a border, strange things had happened along this coast. There had been a proto–Area X.

Some types of omissions made my mind itch as much as more explicit offerings. One journal, half-destroyed by the damp, focused solely on the qualities of a kind of thistle with a lavender blossom that grew in the hinterlands between forest and swamp. Page after page described encountering first one specimen of this thistle and then another, along with minute details about the insects and other creatures that occupied that microhabitat. In no instance did the observer stray more than a foot or two from a particular plant, and at no point, either, did the observer pull back to provide a glimpse of base camp or their own life. After a while, a kind of unease came over me as I began to perceive a terrible presence hovering in the background of these entries. I saw the Crawler or some surrogate approaching in that space just beyond the thistle, and the single focus of the journal keeper a way of coping with that horror. An absence is not a presence, but still with each new depiction of a thistle, a shiver worked deeper and deeper into my spine. When the latter part of the book dissolved into ruined ink and moist pulp, I was almost relieved to be rid of that unnerving repetition, for there had been a hypnotic, trancelike quality to the accounts. If there had been an endless number of pages, I feared that I would have stood there reading for an eternity, until I fell to the floor and died of thirst or starvation.

I began to wonder if the absence of references to the Tower fit this theory as well, this writing around the edges of things.

. . . *in the black water with the sun shining at midnight, those fruit shall come ripe* . . .

Then I found, after several banal or incomprehensible

samples, a journal that wasn't the same type as my own. It dated back to before the first expedition but after the border had come down and referenced "building the wall," which clearly meant the fortification facing the sea. A page later—mixed in with esoteric meteorological readings—three words leapt out at me: "repelling an attack." I read the next few entries with care. The writer at first made no reference to the nature of the attack or the identity of the attackers, but the assault had come from the sea and "left four of us dead," although the wall had held. Later, the sense of desperation grew, and I read:

> . . . the desolation comes from the sea again, along with the strange lights and the marine life that at high tide batters itself against our wall. At night, now, their outliers try to creep in through the gaps in our wall defenses. Still, we hold, but our ammunition is running out. Some of us want to abandon the lighthouse, try for either the island or inland, but the commander says he has his orders. Morale is low. Not everything that is happening to us has a rational explanation.

Soon after, the account trailed off. It had a distinctly unreal quality to it, as if a fictionalized version of a real event. I tried to imagine what Area X might have looked like so long ago. I couldn't.

The lighthouse had drawn expedition members like the ships it had once sought to bring to safety through the narrows and reefs offshore. I could only underscore my previous speculation that to most of them a lighthouse was a symbol, a reassurance of the old order, and by its prominence on the horizon it provided an illusion of a safe refuge. That it had betrayed that trust was manifest in what I had found downstairs. And yet even though some of them must have known that, still they had come. Out of hope. Out of faith. Out of stupidity.

But I had begun to realize that you had to wage a guerrilla war against whatever force had come to inhabit Area X if you wanted to fight at all. You had to fade into the landscape, or like the writer of the thistle chronicles, you had to pretend it wasn't there for as long as possible. To acknowledge it, to try to name it, might be a way of letting it in. (For the same reason, I suppose, I have continued to refer to the changes in me as a "brightness," because to examine this condition too closely—to quantify it or deal with it empirically when I have little control over it—would make it too real.)

At some point, I began to panic at the sheer volume of what remained in front of me, and in my panic I refined my focus further: I would search only for phrases identical to or similar in tone to the words on the wall of the Tower. I started to assail the hill of paper more directly, to wade into the middle sections, the rectangle of light above me a reassurance that this was not the sum of my existence. I rummaged like the rats and the silverfish, I shoved my arms into the mess and came out holding whatever my hands could grasp. At times I lost my balance and became buried in the papers, wrestled with them, my nostrils full of rot, my tongue tasting it. I would have looked unhinged to anyone watching from above, and I knew it even as I engaged in this frenzied, futile activity.

But I found what I was looking for in more journals than I would have expected, and usually it was that beginning phrase: *Where lies the strangling fruit that came from the hand of the sinner I shall bring forth the seeds of the dead to share with the worms* . . . Often it appeared as a scrawled margin note or in other ways disconnected from the text around it. Once, I discovered it documented as a phrase on the wall of the lighthouse itself, which "we quickly washed away," with no reason given. Another time, in a spidery hand, I found a reference to "text in a logbook that reads as if it came out of the Old Testament, but is from no psalm I remember." How could this not refer to the Crawler's writing? . . . *to share with the worms that gather in the darkness and surround the world with the power of their lives* . . . But none of this placed me any closer to understanding *why* or *who*. We were all in the dark, scrabbling at the pile of journals, and if ever I felt the weight of my predecessors, it was there and then, lost in it all.

At a certain point, I discovered I was so overwhelmed I could not continue, could not even go through the motions. It was too much data, served up in too anecdotal a form. I could search those pages for years and perhaps never uncover the right secrets, while caught in a loop of wondering how long this place had existed, who had first left their journals here, why others had followed suit until it had become as inexorable as a long-ingrained ritual. By what impulse, what shared fatalism? All I really thought I knew was that the journals from certain expeditions and certain individual expedition members were missing, that the record was incomplete.

I was also aware that I would have to go back to base camp before nightfall or remain at the lighthouse. I didn't like the idea of traveling in the dark, and if I didn't return, I had no guarantee the surveyor wouldn't abandon me and try to recross the border.

For now, I decided on one last effort. With great difficulty, I climbed to the top of the midden, trying hard not to dislodge journals as I did so. It was a kind of roiling, moving monster beneath my boots, unwilling, like the sand of the dunes outside, to allow my tread without an equal and opposite reaction. But I made it up there anyway.

As I'd imagined, the journals on the top of that mass were more recent, and I immediately found the ones written by members of my husband's expedition. With a kind of lurch in my stomach, I kept rummaging, knowing that it was inevitable what I would stumble upon, and I was right. Stuck to the back of another journal by dried blood or some other substance, I found it more easily than I'd imagined: my husband's journal, written in the confident, bold handwriting I knew from birthday cards, notes on the refrigerator, and shopping lists. The ghost bird had found his ghost, on an inexplicable pile of other ghosts. But rather than looking forward to reading that account, I felt as if I were stealing a private diary that had been locked by his death. A stupid feeling, I know. All he'd ever wanted was for me to open up to him, and as a result he had always been there for the taking. Now, though, I would have to take him as I found him, and it would probably be forever, and I found the truth of that intolerable.

I could not bring myself to read it yet, but fought the urge to throw my husband's journal back on the pile and put it instead with the handful of other journals I planned to take back to base camp with me. I also retrieved two of the psychologist's guns as I climbed up out of that wretched space. I left her other supplies there for now. It might be useful to have a cache in the lighthouse.

It was later than I had thought when I emerged from below, the sky taking on the deep amber hue that marked the beginning of late afternoon. The sea was ablaze with light, but nothing beautiful here fooled me anymore. Human lives had poured into this place over time, volunteered to become party to exile and worse. Under everything lay the ghastly presence of countless desperate struggles. Why did they keep sending us? Why did we keep going? So many lies, so little ability to face the truth. Area X broke minds, I felt, even though it hadn't yet broken mine. A line from a song kept coming back to me: *All this useless knowledge.*

After being in that space for so long, I needed fresh air and the feel of the wind. I dropped what I'd taken into a chair and opened the sliding door to walk out onto the circular ledge bounded by a railing. The wind tore at my clothes and slapped against my face. The sudden chill was cleansing, and the view even better. I could see forever from there. But after a moment, some instinct or premonition made me look straight down, past the remains of the defensive wall, to the beach, part of which was half-hidden by the curve of the dune, the height of the wall, even from that angle.

Emerging from that space was a foot and the end of a leg, amid a flurry of disrupted sand. I trained my binoculars on the foot. It lay unmoving. A familiar pant leg, a familiar boot, with the laces double-tied and even. I gripped the railing tight to counter a feeling of vertigo. I knew the owner of that boot.

It was the psychologist.

04: IMMERSION

Everything I knew about the psychologist came from my observations during training. She had served both as a kind of distant overseer and in a more personal role as our confessor. Except, I had nothing to confess. Perhaps I confessed more under hypnosis, but during our regular sessions, which I had agreed to as a condition of being accepted for the expedition, I volunteered little.

"Tell me about your parents. What are they like?" she would ask, a classic opening gambit.

"Normal," I replied, trying to smile while thinking *distant, impractical, irrelevant, moody, useless.*

"Your mother is an alcoholic, correct? And your father is a kind of . . . con man?"

I almost exhibited a lack of control at what seemed like an insult, not an insight. I almost protested, defiantly, "My mother is an artist and my father is an entrepreneur."

"What are your earliest memories?"

"Breakfast." *A stuffed puppy toy I still have today. Putting a magnifying glass up to an ant lion's sinkhole. Kissing a boy and making him strip for me because I didn't know any better. Falling into a fountain and banging my head; the result, five stitches in the emergency room and an abiding fear of drowning. In the emergency room again when Mom drank too much, followed by the relief of almost a year of sobriety.*

Of all of my answers, "Breakfast" annoyed her the most. I could see it in the corners of her mouth fighting a downward turn, her rigid stance, the coldness in her eyes. But she kept her control.

"Did you have a happy childhood?"

"Normal," I replied. *My mom once so out of it that she poured orange juice into my cereal instead of milk. My dad's incessant, nervous chatter, which made him seem perpetually guilty of something. Cheap motels for vacations by the beach where Mom would cry at the end because we had to go back to the normal strapped-for-cash life, even though we'd never really left it. That sense of impending doom occupying the car.*

"How close were you to your extended family?"

"Close enough." *Birthday cards suitable for a five-year-old even when I was twenty. Visits once every couple of years. A kindly grandfather with long yellow fingernails and the voice of a bear. A grandmother who lectured on the value of religion and saving your pennies. What were their names?*

"How do you feel about being part of a team?"

"Just fine. I've often been part of teams." *And by "part of," I mean off to the side.*

"You were let go from a number of your field jobs. Do you want to tell me why?"

She knew why, so, again, I shrugged and said nothing.

"Are you only agreeing to join this expedition because of your husband?"

"How close were you and your husband?"

"How often did you fight? Why did you fight?"

"Why didn't you call the authorities the moment he returned to your house?"

These sessions clearly frustrated the psychologist on a professional level, on the level of her ingrained training, which was predicated on drawing personal information out of patients in order to establish trust and then delve into deeper issues. But on another level I could never quite grasp, she seemed to approve of my answers. "You're very self-contained," she said once, but not as a pejorative. It was only as we walked for a second day from the border toward base camp that it struck me that perhaps the very qualities she might disapprove of from a psychiatric point of view made me suitable for the expedition.

Now she sat propped up against a mound of sand, sheltered by the shadow of the wall, in a kind of broken pile, one leg straight out, the other trapped beneath her. She was alone. I could see from her condition and the shape of the impact that she had jumped or been pushed from the top of the lighthouse. She probably hadn't quite cleared the wall, been hurt by it on the way down. While I, in my methodical way, had spent hours going through the journals, she had been lying here the whole time. What I couldn't understand was why she was still alive.

Her jacket and shirt were covered in blood, but she was breathing and her eyes were open, looking out toward the ocean as I knelt beside her. She had a gun in her left hand, left arm outstretched, and I gently took the weapon from her, tossed it to the side, just in case.

The psychologist did not seem to register my presence. I touched her gently on one broad shoulder, and then she screamed, lunged away, falling over as I recoiled.

"Annihilation!" she shrieked at me, flailing in confusion. "*Annihilation! Annihilation!*" The word seemed more meaningless the more she repeated it, like the cry of a bird with a broken wing.

"It's just me, the biologist," I said in a calm voice, even though she had rattled me.

"*Just you,*" she said with a wheezing chuckle, as if I'd said something funny. "Just you."

As I propped her up again, I heard a kind of creaking groan and realized she had probably broken most of her ribs. Her left arm and shoulder felt spongy under her jacket. Dark blood was seeping out around her stomach, beneath the hand she had instinctively pressed down on that spot. I could smell that she had pissed herself.

"You're still here," she said, surprise in her voice. "But I killed you, didn't I?" The voice of someone waking from dream or falling into dream.

"Not even a little bit."

A rough wheeze again, and the film of confusion leaving her eyes. "Did you bring water? I'm thirsty."

"I did," and I pressed my canteen to her mouth so she could swallow a few gulps. Drops of blood glistened on her chin.

"Where is the surveyor?" the psychologist asked in a gasp.

"Back at the base camp."

"Wouldn't come with you?"

"No." The wind was blowing back the curls of her hair, revealing a slashing wound on her forehead, possibly from impact with the wall above.

"Didn't like your company?" the psychologist asked. "Didn't like what you've become?"

A chill came over me. "I'm the same as always."

The psychologist's gaze drifted out to sea again. "I saw you, you know, coming down the trail toward the lighthouse. That's how I knew for sure you had changed."

"What did you see?" I asked, to humor her.

A cough, accompanied by red spittle. "You were a *flame*," she said, and I had a brief vision of my brightness, made manifest. "You were a flame, scorching my gaze. A flame drifting across the salt flats, through the ruined village. A slow-burning flame, a will-o'-the-wisp, floating across the marsh and the dunes, floating and floating, like nothing human but something free and floating . . ."

From the shift in her tone, I recognized that even now she was trying to hypnotize me.

"It won't work," I said. "I'm immune to hypnosis now."

Her mouth opened, then closed, then opened again. "Of course you are. You were always difficult," she said, as if talking to a child. Was that an odd sense of pride in her voice?

Perhaps I should have left the psychologist alone, let her die without providing any answers, but I could not find that level of grace within me.

A thought occurred, if I had looked so inhuman: "Why didn't you shoot me dead as I approached?"

An unintentional leer as she swiveled her head to stare at me, unable to control all of the muscles in her face. "My arm, my hand, wouldn't let me pull the trigger."

That sounded delusional to me, and I had seen no sign of an abandoned rifle beside the beacon. I tried again. "And your fall? Pushed or an accident or on purpose?"

A frown appeared, a true perplexity expressed through the network of wrinkles at the corners of her eyes, as if the memory were only coming through in fragments. "I thought . . . I thought something was after me. I tried to shoot you, and couldn't and then you were inside. Then I thought I saw something behind me, coming toward me from the stairs, and I felt such an overwhelming fear I had to get away from it. So I jumped out over the railing. I jumped." As if she couldn't believe she had done such a thing.

"What did the thing coming after you look like?"

A coughing fit, words dribbling out around the edges: "I never saw it. It was never there. Or I saw it too many times. It was inside me. Inside you. I was trying to get away. From what's inside me."

I didn't believe any part of that fragmented explanation at the time, which seemed to imply something had followed her from the Tower. I interpreted the frenzy of her disassociation as part of a need for control. She had lost control of the expedition, and so she had to find someone or something to blame her failure on, no matter how improbable.

I tried a different approach: "Why did you take the anthropologist down into the 'tunnel' in the middle of the night? What happened there?"

She hesitated, but I couldn't tell if it was from caution or because something inside her body was breaking down. Then she said, "A miscalculation. Impatience. I needed intel before we risked the whole mission. I needed to know where we stood."

"You mean, the progress of the Crawler?"

She smiled wickedly. "Is that what you call it? The Crawler?"

"What happened?" I asked.

"What do you think happened? It all went wrong. The anthropologist got too close." Translation: The psychologist had forced her to get close. "The thing *reacted*. It killed her, wounded me."

"Which is why you looked so shaken the next morning."

"Yes. And because I could tell that you were already changing."

"I'm not changing!" I shouted it, an unexpected rage rising inside of me.

A wet chuckle, a mocking tone. "Of course you're not. You're just becoming more of what you've always been. And I'm not changing, either. None of us are changing. Everything is fine. Let's have a picnic."

"Shut up. Why did you abandon us?"

"The expedition had been compromised."

"That isn't an explanation."

"Did you ever give *me* a proper explanation, during training?"

"We hadn't been compromised, not enough to abandon the mission."

"Sixth day after reaching base camp and one person is dead, two already *changing*, the fourth wavering? I would call that a disaster."

"If it was a disaster, you helped create it." I realized that as much as I mistrusted the psychologist personally, I had come to rely on her to lead the expedition. On some level, I was furious that she had betrayed us, furious that she might be leaving me now. "You just panicked, and you gave up."

The psychologist nodded. "That, too. I did. I did. I should have recognized earlier that you had changed. I should have sent you back to the border. I shouldn't have gone down there with the anthropologist. But here we are." She grimaced, coughed out a thick wetness.

I ignored the jab, changed the line of questioning. "What does the border look like?"

That smile again. "I'll tell you when I get there."

"What really happens when we cross over?"

"Not what you might expect."

"Tell me! What do we cross through?" I felt as if I were getting lost. Again.

There was a gleam in her eye now that I did not like, that promised damage. "I want you to think about something. You might be immune to hypnosis—you might—but what about the veil already in place? What if I removed that veil so you could access your own memories of crossing the border?" the psychologist asked. "Would you like that, Little Flame? Would you like it or would you go mad?"

"If you try to do anything to me, I'll kill you," I said—and meant it. The thought of hypnosis in general, and the conditioning behind it, had been difficult for me, an invasive price to be paid in return for access to Area X. The thought of further tampering was intolerable.

"How many of your memories do you think are implanted?" the psychologist asked. "How many of your memories of the world beyond the border are verifiable?"

"That won't work on me," I told her. "I am sure of the here and now, this moment, and the next. I am sure of my past."

That was ghost bird's castle keep, and it was inviolate. It might have been punctured by the hypnosis during training, but it had not been breached. Of this I was certain, and would continue to be certain, because I had no choice.

"I'm sure your husband felt the same way before the end," the psychologist said.

I sat back on my haunches, staring at her. I wanted to leave her before she poisoned me, but I couldn't.

"Let's stick to your own hallucinations," I said. "Describe the Crawler to me."

"There are things you must see with your own eyes. You might get closer. You might be more familiar to it." Her lack of regard for the anthropologist's fate was hideous, but so was mine.

"What did you hide from us about Area X?"

"Too general a question." I think it amused the psychologist, even dying, for me to so desperately need answers from her.

"Okay, then: What do the black boxes measure?"

"Nothing. They don't measure anything. It's just a psychological ploy to keep the expedition calm: no red light, no danger."

"What is the secret behind the Tower?"

"The tunnel? If we knew, do you think we would keep sending in expeditions?"

"They're scared. The Southern Reach."

"That is my impression."

"Then they have no answers."

"I'll give you this scrap: The border is advancing. For now, slowly, a little bit more every year. In ways you wouldn't expect. But maybe soon it'll eat a mile or two at a time."

The thought of that silenced me for a long moment. When you are too close to the center of a mystery there is no way to pull back and see the shape of it entire. The black boxes might do nothing but in my mind they were all blinking red.

"How many expeditions have there been?"

"Ah, the journals," she said. "There are quite a lot of them, aren't there?"

"That doesn't answer my question."

"Maybe I don't know the answer. Maybe I just don't want to tell you."

It was going to continue this way, to the end, and there wasn't anything I could do about it.

"What did the 'first' expedition really find?"

The psychologist grimaced, and not from her pain this time, but more as if she were remembering something that caused her shame. "There's video from that expedition . . . of a sort. The main reason no advanced tech was allowed after that."

Video. Somehow, after searching through the mound of journals, that information didn't startle me. I kept moving forward.

"What orders didn't you reveal to us?"

"You're beginning to bore me. And I'm beginning to fade a little . . . Sometimes we tell you more, sometimes less. They have their metrics and their reasons." Somehow the "they" felt made of cardboard, as if she didn't quite believe in "them."

Reluctantly, I returned to the personal. "What do you know about my husband?"

"Nothing more than you'll find out from reading his journal. Have you found it yet?"

"No," I lied.

"Very insightful—about you, especially."

Was that a bluff? She'd certainly had enough time up in the lighthouse to find it, read it, and toss it back onto the pile.

It didn't matter. The sky was darkening and encroaching, the waves deepening, the surf making the shorebirds scatter on their stilt legs and then regroup as it receded. The sand seemed suddenly more porous around us. The meandering paths of crabs and worms continued to be written into its surface. A whole community lived here, was going about its business, oblivious to our conversation. And where out there lay the seaward border? When I had asked the psychologist during training she had said only that no one had ever crossed it, and I had imagined expeditions that just evaporated into mist and light and distance.

A rattle had entered the psychologist's breathing, which was now shallow and inconsistent.

"Is there anything I can do to make you more comfortable?" Relenting.

"Leave me here when I die," she said. Now all her fear was visible. "Don't bury me. Don't take me anywhere. Leave me here where I belong."

"Is there anything else you're willing to tell me?"

"We should never have come here. I should never have come here." The rawness in her tone hinted at a personal anguish that went beyond her physical condition.

"That's all?"

"I've come to believe it is the one fundamental truth."

I took her to mean that it was better to let the border advance, to ignore it, let it affect some other, more distant generation. I didn't agree with her, but I said nothing. Later, I would come to believe she had meant something altogether different.

"Has anyone ever really come back from Area X?"

"Not for a long time now," the psychologist said in a tired whisper. "Not really." But I don't know if she had heard the question.

Her head sagged downward and she lost consciousness, then came to again and stared out at the waves. She muttered a few words, one of which might have been "remote" or "demote" and another that might have been "hatching" or "watching." But I could not be sure.

Soon dusk would descend. I gave her more water. It was hard to think of her as an adversary the closer she came to death, even though clearly she knew so much more than she had told me. Regardless, it didn't bear much thought because she wasn't going to divulge anything else. And maybe I *had* looked to her like a flame as I came near. Maybe that was the only way she could think of me now.

"Did you know about the pile of journals?" I asked. "Before we came here?"

But she did not answer.

There were things I had to do after she died, even though I was running short of daylight, even though I did not like doing them. If she wouldn't answer my questions while alive, then she would have to answer some of them now. I took off the psychologist's jacket and laid it to the side, discovering in the process that she had hidden her own journal in a zippered inside pocket, folded up. I put that to the side, too, under a stone, the pages flapping in the gusts of wind.

Then I took out my penknife and, with great care, cut away the left sleeve of her shirt. The sponginess of her shoulder had bothered me, and I saw I'd had good reason to be concerned. From her collarbone down to her elbow, her arm had been colonized by a fibrous green-gold fuzziness, which gave off a faint glow. From the indentations and long rift running down her triceps, it appeared to have spread from an initial wound—the wound she said she had received from the Crawler. Whatever had contaminated me, this different and more direct contact had spread faster and had more disastrous consequences. Certain parasites and fruiting bodies could cause not just paranoia but schizophrenia, all-too-realistic hallucinations, and thus promote delusional behavior. I had no doubt now that she had seen me as a flame approaching, that she had attributed her inability to shoot me to some exterior force, that she had been assailed by the fear of some approaching presence. If nothing else, the memory of the encounter with the Crawler would, I imagined, have unhinged her to some degree.

I cut a skin sample from her arm, along with some of the flesh beneath, and prodded it into a collection vial. Then I took another sample from her other arm. Once I got back to base camp, I would examine both.

I was shaking a little by then, so I took a break, turned my attention to the journal. It was devoted to transcribing the words on the wall of the Tower, was filled with so many new passages:

*. . . but whether it decays under the earth or above on green
fields, or out to sea or in the very air, all shall come to revelation, and to revel, in the knowledge of the strangling fruit
and the hand of the sinner shall rejoice, for there is no sin
in shadow or in light that the seeds of the dead cannot
forgive . . .*

There were a few notes scribbled in the margins. One
read "lighthouse keeper," which made me wonder if she'd
circled the man in the photograph. Another read "North?"
and a third "island." I had no clue what these notes meant—
or what it said about the psychologist's state of mind that her
journal was devoted to this text. I felt only a simple, uncom-
plicated relief that someone had completed a task for me
that would have been laborious and difficult otherwise. My
only question was whether she had gotten the text from the
walls of the Tower, from journals within the lighthouse, or
from some other source entirely. I still don't know.

Careful to avoid contact with her shoulder and arm, I
then searched the psychologist's body. I patted down her
shirt, her pants, searching for anything hidden. I found a
tiny handgun strapped to her left calf and a letter in a small
envelope folded up in her right boot. The psychologist had
written a name on the envelope; at least, it looked like her
handwriting. The name started with an S. Was it her child's
name? A friend? A lover? I had not seen a name or heard a
name spoken aloud for months, and seeing one now bothered
me deeply. It seemed wrong, as if it did not belong in Area
X. A name was a dangerous luxury here. Sacrifices didn't
need names. People who served a function didn't need to be
named. In all ways, the name was a further and unwanted

confusion to me, a dark space that kept growing and growing in my mind.

I tossed the gun far across the sand, balled up the envelope, sent it after the gun. I was thinking of having discovered my husband's journal, and how in some ways that discovery was worse than its absence. And, on some level, I was still angry at the psychologist.

Finally I searched her pants pockets. I found some change, a smooth worry stone, and a slip of paper. On the paper I found a list of hypnotic suggestions that included "induce paralysis," "induce acceptance," and "compel obedience," each corresponding to an activation word or phrase. She must have been intensely afraid of forgetting which words gave her control over us, to have written them down. Her cheat sheet included other reminders, like: "Surveyor needs reinforcement" and "Anthropologist's mind is porous." About me she had only this cryptic phrase: "Silence creates its own violence." How insightful.

The word "Annihilation" was followed by "help induce immediate suicide."

We had all been given self-destruct buttons, but the only one who could push them was dead.

Part of my husband's life had been defined by nightmares he'd had as a child. These debilitating experiences had sent him to a psychiatrist. They involved a house and a basement and the awful crimes that had occurred there. But the psychiatrist had ruled out suppressed memory, and he was left at the end with just trying to draw the poison by keeping a diary about them. Then, as an adult at university, a few months before he'd joined the navy, he had gone to a classic film festival . . . and there, up on the big screen, my future husband had seen his nightmares acted out. It was only then that he realized the television set must have been left on at some point when he was only a couple of years old, with that horror movie playing. The splinter in his mind, never fully dislodged, disintegrated into nothing. He said that was the moment he knew he was free, that it was from then on that he left behind the shadows of his childhood . . . because it had all been an illusion, a fake, a forgery, a scrawling across his mind that had falsely made him go in one direction when he had been meant to go in another.

"I've had a kind of dream for a while now," he confessed to me the night he told me he had agreed to join the eleventh expedition. "A new one, and not really a nightmare this time."

In these dreams, he floated over a pristine wilderness as if from the vantage point of a marsh hawk, and the feeling of freedom "is indescribable. It's as if you took everything from my nightmares and reversed it." As the dreams progressed and repeated, they varied in their intensity and their viewpoint. Some nights he swam through the marsh canals. Others, he became a tree or a drop of water. Everything he experienced refreshed him. Everything he experienced made him want to go to Area X.

Although he couldn't tell me much, he confessed that he already had met several times with people who recruited for the expeditions. That he had talked to them for hours, that he knew this was the right decision. It was an honor. Not everyone was taken—some were rejected and others lost the thread along the way. Still others, I pointed out to him, must have wondered what they had done, after it was too late. All I understood of what he called Area X at the time came from the vague official story of environmental catastrophe, along with rumors and sideways whispers. Danger? I'm not sure this crossed my mind so much as the idea that my husband had just told me he wanted to leave me and had withheld the information for weeks. I was not yet privy to the idea of hypnosis or reconditioning, so it did not occur to me that he might have been *made suggestible* during his meetings.

My response was a profound silence as he searched my face for what he thought he hoped to find there. He turned away, sat on the couch, while I poured myself a very large glass of wine and took the chair opposite him. We remained that way for a long time.

A little later, he started to talk again—about what he knew of Area X, about how his work right now wasn't fulfilling, how he needed more of a challenge. But I wasn't really listening. I was thinking about my mundane job. I was thinking about the wilderness. I was wondering why I hadn't done something like he was doing now: dreaming of another place, and how to get there. In that moment, I couldn't blame him, not really. Didn't I sometimes go off on field trips for my job? I might not be gone for months, but in principle it was the same thing.

The arguing came later, when it became real to me. But never pleading. I never begged him to stay. I couldn't do that. Perhaps he even thought that going away would save our marriage, that somehow it would bring us closer together. I don't know. I have no clue. Some things I will never be good at.

But as I stood beside the psychologist's body looking out

to sea, I knew that my husband's journal waited for me, that soon I would know what sort of nightmare he had encountered here. And I knew, too, that I still blamed him fiercely for his decision . . . and yet even so, somewhere in the heart of me I had begun to believe there was no place I would rather be than in Area X.

I had lingered too long and would have to travel through the dark to make it back to base camp. If I kept up a steady pace, I might make it back by midnight. There was some advantage in arriving at an unexpected hour, given how I had left things with the surveyor. Something also warned me against staying at the lighthouse overnight. Perhaps it was just the unease from seeing the strangeness of the psychologist's wound or perhaps I still felt as if a presence inhabited that place, but regardless I set out soon after gathering up my knapsack full of supplies and my husband's journal. Behind me lay the increasingly solemn silhouette of what was no longer really a lighthouse but instead a kind of reliquary. As I stared back, I saw a thin green fountain of light gushing up, framed by the curve of the dunes, and felt even more resolve to put miles between us. It was the psychologist's wound, from where she lay on the beach, glowing more brightly than before. The suggestion of some sped-up form of life burning fiercely did not bear close scrutiny. Another phrase I had seen copied in her journal came to mind: *There shall be a fire that knows your name, and in the presence of the strangling fruit, its dark flame shall acquire every part of you.*

Within the hour, the lighthouse had disappeared into the night, and with it the beacon the psychologist had become. The wind picked up, the darkness intensified. The ever-more distant sound of waves was like eavesdropping on a sinister, whispering conversation. I walked as quietly as possible through the ruined village under just a sliver of moon, unwilling to risk my flashlight. The shapes in the exposed remains of rooms had gathered a darkness about them that stood out against the night and in their utter stillness I sensed an unnerving suggestion of movement. I was glad to soon be past them and onto the part of the trail where the reeds choked both the canal on the seaward side and the little lakes to the left. In a while, I would encounter the black water and cypress trees, vanguard for the sturdy utility of the pines.

A few minutes later, the moaning started. For a moment I thought it was in my head. Then I stopped abruptly, stood there listening. Whatever we had heard every night at dusk was at it again, and in my eagerness to leave the lighthouse I had forgotten it lived in the reeds. This close the sound was more guttural, filled with confused anguish and rage. It seemed so utterly human and inhuman, that, for the second time since entering Area X, I considered the supernatural. The sound came from ahead of me and from the landward side, through the thick reeds that kept the water away from the sides of the trail. It seemed unlikely I could pass by without it hearing me. And what then?

Finally I decided to forge ahead. I took out the smaller of my two flashlights and crouched as I turned it on so the beam couldn't easily be seen above the reeds. In this awkward way, I walked forward, gun drawn in my other hand, alert to the direction of the sound. Soon I could hear it closer, if still distant, pushing through the reeds as it continued its horrible moaning.

A few minutes passed, and I made good progress. Then, abruptly, something nudged against my boot, flopped over. I aimed my flashlight at the ground—and leapt back, gasping. Incredibly, a human face seemed to be rising out of the earth. But when after a moment nothing further happened, I shone my light on it again and saw it was a kind of tan mask made of skin, half-transparent, resembling in its way the discarded shell of a horseshoe crab. A wide face, with a hint of pockmarks across the left cheek. The eyes were blank, sightless, staring. I felt as if I should recognize these features— that it was very important—but with them disembodied in this way, I could not.

Somehow the sight of this mask restored to me a measure of the calm that I had lost during my conversation with the psychologist. No matter how strange, a discarded exoskeleton, even if part of it resembled a human face, represented a kind of solvable mystery. One that, for the moment at least, pushed back the disturbing image of an expanding border and the countless lies told by the Southern Reach.

When I bent at the knees and shone my flashlight ahead, I saw more detritus from a kind of molting: a long trail of skin-like debris, husks, and sloughings. Clearly I might soon meet what had shed this material, and just as clearly the moaning creature was, or had once been, human.

I recalled the deserted village, the strange eyes of the dolphins. A question existed there that I might in time answer in too personal a way. But the most important question in that moment was whether just after molting the thing became sluggish or more active. It depended on the species, and I was not an expert on this one. Nor did I have much stamina left for a new encounter, even though it was too late to retreat.

Continuing on, I came to a place on the left where the reeds had been flattened, veering off to form a path about three feet wide. The moltings, if that's what they were, veered off, too. Shining my flashlight down the path, I could see it curved sharply right after less than a hundred feet. This meant that the creature was already ahead of me, out in the reeds, and could possibly circle back and emerge to block my path back to base camp.

The dragging sounds had intensified, almost equal to the moaning. A thick musk clung to the air.

I still had no desire to return to the lighthouse, so I picked up my pace. Now the darkness was so complete I could only see a few feet ahead of me, the flashlight revealing little or nothing. I felt as if I were moving through an encircling tunnel. The moaning grew still louder, but I could not determine its direction. The smell became a special kind of stench. The ground began to sag a little under my weight, and I knew water must be close.

There came the moaning again, as close as I'd ever heard it, but now mixed with a loud thrashing sound. I stopped and stood on tiptoe to shine my flashlight over the reeds to my left in time to see a great disrupting wave of motion ahead at a right angle to the trail, and closing fast. A dislocation of the reeds, a fast smashing that made them fall as if machine-threshed. The thing was trying to outflank me, and the brightness within surged to cover my panic.

I hesitated for just a moment. Some part of me wanted to see the creature, after having heard it for so many days.

Was it the remnants of the scientist in me, trying to regroup, trying to apply logic when all that mattered was survival?

If so, it was a very small part.

I ran. It surprised me how fast I could run—I'd never had to run that fast before. Down the tunnel of blackness lined with reeds, raked by them and not caring, willing the brightness to propel me forward. To get past the beast before it cut me off. I could feel the thudding vibration of its passage, the rasping clack of the reeds beneath its tread, and there was a kind of expectant tone to its moaning now that sickened me with the urgency of its seeking.

From out of the darkness there came an impression of a great weight, aimed at me from my left. A suggestion of the side of a tortured, pale visage and a great, ponderous bulk behind it. Barreling toward a point ahead of me, and me with no choice but to let it keep coming, lunging forward like a sprinter at the finish line, so I could be past it and free.

It was coming so fast, too fast. I could tell I wasn't going to make it, couldn't possibly make it, not at that angle, but I was committed now.

The crucial moment came. I thought I felt its hot breath on my side, flinched and cried out even as I ran. But then the way was clear, and from almost right behind I heard a high keening, and the feeling of the space, the air, suddenly *filled*, and the sound of something massive trying to brake, trying to change direction, and being pulled into the reeds on the opposite side of the trail by its own momentum. An almost plaintive keening, a lonely sound in that place, called out to me. And kept calling, pleading with me to return, to see it entire, to acknowledge its existence.

I did not look back. I kept running.

Eventually, gasping for air, I stopped. On rubbery legs I walked until the trail opened up into forest lands, far enough to find a large oak I could climb, and spent the night in an uncomfortable position wedged into a crook of the tree. If the moaning creature had followed me there, I don't know what I would have done. I could still hear it, though far distant again. I did not want to think about it, but I could not stop thinking about it.

I drifted in and out of sleep, one watchful eye on the ground. Once, something large and snuffling paused at the base of the tree, but then went on its way. Another time, I had the sense of vague shapes moving in the middle distance, but nothing came of it. They seemed to stop for a moment, luminous eyes floating in the dark, but I sensed no threat from them. I held my husband's journal to my chest like a talisman to ward off the night, still refusing to open it. My fears about what it might contain had only grown.

Sometime before morning, I woke again to find that my brightness had become literal: My skin gave off a faint phosphorescence against the darkness, and I tried to hide my hands in my sleeves, draw my collar up high, so I would be less visible, then drifted off again. Part of me just wanted to sleep forever, through the rest of anything that might occur.

But I did remember one thing, now: where I had seen the molted mask before—the psychologist from the eleventh expedition, a man I had seen interviewed after his return across the border. A man who had said, in a calm and even tone, "It was quite beautiful, quite peaceful in Area X. We saw nothing unusual. Nothing at all." And then had smiled in a vague way.

Death, as I was beginning to understand it, was not the same thing here as back across the border.

The next morning my head was still full of the moans of the creature as I reentered the part of Area X where the trail rose to a steep incline, and on either side the swampy black water was littered with the deceptively dead-seeming cypress knees. The water stole all sound, and its unmoving surface reflected back only gray moss and tree limbs. I loved this part of the trail as I loved no other. Here the world had a watchfulness matched only by a sense of peaceful solitude. The stillness was simultaneously an invitation to let down your guard and a rebuke against letting down your guard. Base camp was a mile away, and I was lazy with the light and the hum of insects in the tall grass. I was already rehearsing what I would say to the surveyor, what I would tell her and what I would withhold.

The brightness within me flared up. I had time to take a half step to the right.

The first shot took me in the left shoulder instead of the heart, and the impact twisted me as it pushed me back. The second shot ripped through my left side, not so much lifting me off my feet as making me spin and trip myself. Into the profound silence as I hit the incline and jounced down the hill there came a roaring in my ears. I lay at the bottom of the hill, breath knocked out of me, one outstretched hand plunged into the black water and the other arm trapped beneath me. The pain in my left side seemed at first as if someone kept opening me up with a butcher knife and sewing me back together. But it quickly subsided to a kind of roiling ache, the bullet wounds reduced through some cellular conspiracy to a sensation like the slow squirming inside me of tiny animals.

Only seconds had passed. I knew I had to move. Luckily, my gun had been holstered or it would have gone flying. I took it out now. I had seen the scope, a tiny circle in the tall grass, recognized who had set the ambush. The surveyor was ex-military, and good, but she couldn't know that the brightness had protected me, that shock wasn't overtaking me, that the wound hadn't transfixed me with paralyzing pain.

I rolled onto my belly, intending to crawl along the water's edge.

Then I heard the surveyor's voice, calling out to me from the other side of the embankment: "Where is the psychologist? What did you do with her?"

I made the mistake of telling the truth.

"She's dead," I called back, trying to make my voice sound shaky and weak.

The surveyor's only reply was to fire a round over my head, perhaps hoping I'd break cover.

"I didn't kill the psychologist," I shouted. "She jumped from the top of the lighthouse."

"*Risk for reward!*" the surveyor responded, throwing it back at me like a grenade. She must have thought about that moment the whole time I'd been gone. It had no more effect on me than had my attempt to use it on her.

"Listen to me! You've hurt me—badly. You can leave me out here. I'm not your enemy."

Pathetic words, placating words. I waited, but the surveyor didn't reply. There was just the buzzing of the bees around the wildflowers, a gurgling of water somewhere in the black swamp beyond the embankment. I looked up at the stunning blue of the sky and wondered if it was time to start moving.

"Go back to base camp, take the supplies," I shouted, trying again. "Return to the border. I don't care. I won't stop you."

"I don't believe you about any of it!" she shouted, the voice a little closer, advancing along the other side. Then: "You've come back and you're not human anymore. You should kill yourself so I don't have to." I didn't like her casual tone.

"I'm as human as you," I replied. "This is a natural thing," and realized she wouldn't understand that I was referring to the brightness. I wanted to say that I was a natural thing, too, but I didn't know the truth of that—and none of this was helping plead my case anyway.

"Tell me your name!" she screamed. "Tell me your name! *Tell me your goddamn fucking name!*"

"That won't make any difference," I shouted back. "How would that make any difference? I don't understand why that makes a difference."

Silence was my answer. She would speak no more. I was a demon, a devil, something she couldn't understand or had chosen not to. I could feel her coming ever closer, crouching for cover.

She wouldn't fire again until she had a clear shot, whereas I had the urge to just charge her, firing wildly. Instead, I half crawled, half crept *toward* her, fast along the water's edge.

She might expect me to get away by putting distance between us, but I knew with the range of her rifle that was suicidal. I tried to slow my breathing. I wanted to be able to hear any sound she might make, giving away her position.

After a moment, I heard footsteps opposite me on the other side of the hill. I found a clump of muddy earth, and I lobbed it low and long down the edge of the black water, back the way I had come. As it was landing about fifty feet from me with a glutinous plop, I was edging my way up the hillside so I could just barely see the edge of the trail.

The top of the surveyor's head rose up not ten feet ahead of me. She had dropped down to crawl through the long grass of the path. It was just a momentary glimpse. She was in plain view for less than a second, and then would be gone. I didn't think. I didn't hesitate. I shot her.

Her head jolted to the side and she slumped soundlessly into the grass and turned over on her back with a groan, as if she had been disturbed in her sleep, and then lay still. The side of her face was covered with blood and her forehead looked grotesquely misshapen. I slid back down the incline. I was staring at my gun, shocked. I felt as if I were stuck between two futures, even though I had already made the decision to live in one of them. Now it was just me.

When I checked again, cautious and low against the side of the hill, I saw her still sprawled there, unmoving. I had never killed anyone before. I was not sure, given the logic of this place, that I had truly killed someone now. At least, this was what I told myself to control my shakes. Because behind it all, I kept thinking that I could have tried to reason with her a little longer, or not taken the shot and escaped into the wilderness.

I got up and made my way up the hill, feeling sore all over although my shoulder remained just a dull ache. Standing over the body, her rifle lying straight above her bloody head like an exclamation mark, I wondered what her last hours had been like at base camp. What doubts had racked her. If she had started back to the border, hesitated, returned to the camp, set out again, caught in a circle of indecision. Surely some trigger had driven her to confront me, or perhaps living alone in her own head overnight in this place had been enough. Solitude could press down on a person, seem to demand that action be taken. If I had come back when I'd promised, might it all have been different?

I couldn't leave her there, but I hesitated about taking her back to base camp and burying her in the old graveyard behind the tents. The brightness within me made me unsure. What if there was a purpose for her in this place? Would burying her circumvent an ability to change that might belong to her, even now? Finally I rolled her over and over, the skin still elastic and warm, blood spooling out from the wound in her head, until she reached the water's edge. Then I said a few words about how I hoped she would forgive me, and how I forgave her for shooting at me. I don't know if my words made much sense to either of us at that point. It all sounded absurd to me as I said it. If she had suddenly been resurrected we would probably both admit we forgave nothing.

Carrying her in my arms, I waded into the black water. I let her go when I was knee-deep and watched her sink. When I could no longer see even the outstretched pale anemone of her left hand, I waded back to shore. I did not know if she was religious, expected to be resurrected in heaven or become food for the worms. But regardless, the cypress trees formed a kind of cathedral over her as she went deeper and deeper.

I had no time to absorb what had just happened, however. Soon after I stood once again on the trail, the brightness usurped many more places than just my nerve centers. I crumpled to the ground cocooned in what felt like an encroaching winter of dark ice, the brightness spreading into a corona of brilliant blue light with a white core. It felt like cigarette burns as a kind of searing snow drifted down and infiltrated my skin. Soon I became so frozen, so utterly numb, trapped there on the trail in my own body, that my eyes became fixed on the thick blades of grass in front of me, my mouth half open in the dirt. There should have been an awareness of comfort at being spared the pain of my wounds, but I was being haunted in my delirium.

I can remember only three moments from these hauntings. In the first, the surveyor, psychologist, and anthropologist peered down at me through ripples as if I were a tadpole staring up through a pool of water. They kept staring for an abnormally long time. In the second, I sat beside the moaning creature, my hand upon its head as I murmured something in a language I did not understand. In the third, I stared at a living map of the border, which had been depicted as if it were a great circular moat surrounding Area X. In that moat vast sea creatures swam, oblivious to me watching them; I could feel the absence of their regard like a kind of terrible bereavement.

All that time, I discovered later from thrash marks in the grass, I wasn't frozen at all: I was spasming and twitching in the dirt like a worm, some distant part of me still experiencing the agony, trying to die because of it, even though the brightness wouldn't let that happen. If I could have reached my gun, I think I would have shot myself in the head . . . and been glad of it.

◈

It may be clear by now that I am not always good at telling people things they feel they have a right to know, and in this account thus far I have neglected to mention some details about the brightness. My reason for this is, again, the hope that any reader's initial opinion in judging my objectivity might not be influenced by these details. I have tried to compensate by revealing more personal information than I would otherwise, in part because of its relevance to the nature of Area X.

The truth is that in the moments before the surveyor tried to kill me, the brightness expanded within me to enhance my senses, and I could feel the shifting of the surveyor's hips as she lay against the ground and zeroed in on me through the scope. I could hear the sound of the beads of sweat as they trickled down her forehead. I could smell the deodorant she wore, and I could taste the yellowing grass she had flattened to set her ambush. When I shot her, it was with these enhanced senses still at work, and that was the only reason she was vulnerable to me.

This was, in extremis, a sudden exaggeration of what I had been experiencing already. On the way to the lighthouse and back, the brightness had manifested in part as a low-grade cold. I had run a mild fever, had coughed, and had sinus difficulties. I had felt faint at times and light-headed. A floating sensation and a heaviness had run through my body at intervals, never with any balance, so that I was either buoyant or dragging.

My husband would have been proactive about the brightness. He would have found a thousand ways to try to cure it—and to take away the scars, too—and not let me deal with it on my own terms, which is why during our time together I sometimes didn't tell him when I was sick. But in this case, anyway, all of that effort on his part would have been pointless. You can either waste time worrying about a death that might not come or concentrate on what's left to you.

When I finally returned to my senses it was already noon of the next day. Somehow I had managed to drag myself back to base camp. I was wrung out, a husk that needed to gulp down almost a gallon of water over the next hours to feel whole. My side burned, but I could tell that too-quick repair was taking place, enough for me to move about. The brightness, which had already infiltrated my limbs, now seemed in one final surge to have been fought to a draw by my body, its progress stunted by the need to tend to my injuries. The cold symptoms had receded and the lightness, the heaviness, had been replaced by a constant sustaining hum within me and for a time an unsettling sensation, as of something creeping under my skin, forming a layer that perfectly mimicked the one that could be seen.

I knew not to trust this feeling of well-being, that it could simply be the interregnum before another stage. Any relief that thus far the changes seemed no more radical than enhanced senses and reflexes and a phosphorescent tint to my skin paled before what I had now learned: To keep the brightness in check, I would have to continue to become wounded, to be injured. To shock my system.

In that context, when confronted with the chaos that was base camp my attitude was perhaps more prosaic than it might have been otherwise. The surveyor had hacked at the tents until long strips of the tough canvas fabric hung loose. The remaining records of scientific data left by prior expeditions had been burned; I could still see blackened fragments sticking out of the ash-crumbling logs. Any weapons she had been unable to carry with her she had destroyed by carefully taking them apart piece by piece; then she had scattered the pieces all around the camp as if to challenge me. Emptied-out cans of food lay strewn and gaping across the entire area. In my absence, the surveyor had become a kind of frenzied serial killer of the inanimate.

Her journal lay like an enticement on the remains of her bed in her tent, surrounded by a flurry of maps, some old and yellowing. But it was blank. Those few times I had seen her, apart from us, "writing" in it had been a deception. She had never had any intention of letting the psychologist or any of us know her true thoughts. I found I respected that.

Still, she had left one final, pithy statement, on a piece of paper by the bed, which perhaps helped explain her hostility: "The anthropologist tried to come back, but I took care of her." She had either been crazy or all too sane. I carefully sorted through the maps, but they were not of Area X. She had written things on them, personal things that spoke to remembrance, until I realized that the maps must show places she had visited or lived. I could not fault her for returning to them, for searching for something from the past that might anchor her in the present, no matter how futile that quest.

As I explored the remains of base camp further, I took

stock of my situation. I found a few cans of food she had somehow overlooked. She also had missed some of the drinking water because, as I always did, I had secreted some of it in my sleeping bag. Although all of my samples were gone— these I imagined she'd flung into the black swamp on her way back down the trail to set her ambush—nothing had been solved or helped by this behavior. I kept my measurements and observations about samples in a small notebook in my knapsack. I would miss my larger, more powerful microscope, but the one I'd packed would do. I had enough food to last me a couple of weeks as I did not eat much. My water would last another three or four days beyond that, and I could always boil more. I had enough matches to keep a fire going for a month, and the skills to create one without matches anyway. More supplies awaited me in the lighthouse, at the very least in the psychologist's knapsack.

Out back, I saw what the surveyor had added to the old graveyard: an empty, newly dug grave with a mound of dirt out to the side—and stabbed into the ground, a simple cross made from fallen branches. Had the grave been meant to hold me or the anthropologist? Or both? I did not like the idea of lying next to the anthropologist for all eternity.

Cleaning up a little later, a fit of laughter came out of nowhere and made me double up in pain. I had suddenly remembered doing the dishes after dinner the night my husband had come back from across the border. I could distinctly recall wiping the spaghetti and chicken scraps from a plate and wondering with a kind of bewilderment how such a mundane act could coexist with the mystery of his reappearance.

05: DISSOLUTION

I have never done well in cities, even though I lived in one by necessity—because my husband needed to be there, because the best jobs for me were there, because I had self-destructed when I'd had opportunities in the field. But I was not a domesticated animal. The dirt and grit of a city, the unending *wakefulness* of it, the crowdedness, the constant light obscuring the stars, the omnipresent gasoline fumes, the thousand ways it presaged our destruction . . . none of these things appealed to me.

"Where do you go so late at night?" my husband had asked several times, about nine months before he left as part of the eleventh expedition. There was an unspoken "really" before the "go"—I could hear it, loud and insistent.

"Nowhere," I said. *Everywhere.*

"No, really—where do you go?" It was to his credit that he had never tried to follow me.

"I'm not cheating on you if that's what you mean."

The directness of that usually stopped him, even if it didn't reassure him.

I had told him a late-night walk alone relaxed me, allowed me to sleep when the stress or boredom of my job became too much. But in truth I didn't walk except the distance to an empty lot overgrown with grass. The empty lot appealed to me because it wasn't truly empty. Two species of snail called it home and three species of lizard, along with butter-flies and dragonflies. From lowly origins—a muddy rut from truck tires—a puddle had over time collected rain-water to become a pond. Fish eggs had found their way to that place, and minnows and tadpoles could be seen there, and aquatic insects. Weeds had grown up around it, making the soil less likely to erode into the water. Songbirds on mi-gration used it as a refueling station.

As habitats went, the lot wasn't complex, but its proxim-ity dulled the impulse in me to just get in a car and start driving for the nearest wild place. I liked to visit late at night because I might see a wary fox passing through or catch a sugar glider resting on a telephone pole. Nighthawks gathered nearby to feast off the insects bombarding the streetlamps. Mice and owls played out ancient rituals of predator and prey. They all had a watchfulness about them that was different from animals in true wilderness; this was a jaded watchful-ness, the result of a long and weary history. Tales of bad-faith encounters in human-occupied territory, tragic past events.

I didn't tell my husband my walk had a destination because I wanted to keep the lot for myself. There are so many things couples do from habit and because they are expected to, and I didn't mind those rituals. Sometimes I even enjoyed them. But I needed to be selfish about that patch of urban wilderness. It expanded in my mind while I was at work, calmed me, gave me a series of miniature dramas to look forward to. I didn't know that while I was applying this Band-Aid to my need to be unconfined, my husband was dreaming of Area X and much greater open spaces. But, later, the parallel helped assuage my anger at his leaving, and then my confusion when he came back in such a changed form . . . even if the stark truth is that I still did not truly understand what I had missed about him.

The psychologist had said, "The border is advancing . . . a little bit more every year."

But I found that statement too limiting, too ignorant. There were thousands of "dead" spaces like the lot I had observed, thousands of transitional environments that no one saw, that had been rendered invisible because they were not "of use." Anything could inhabit them for a time without anyone noticing. We had come to think of the border as this monolithic invisible wall, but if members of the eleventh expedition had been able to return without our noticing, couldn't other things have already gotten through?

In this new phase of my brightness, recovering from my wounds, the Tower called incessantly to me; I could feel its physical presence under the earth with a clarity that mimicked that first flush of attraction, when you knew without looking exactly where the object of desire stood in the room. Part of this was my own need to return, but part might be due to the effect of the spores, and so I fought it because I had work to do first. This work might also, if I was left to it without any strange intercession, put everything in perspective.

To start with, I had to quarantine the lies and obfuscation of my superiors from data that pertained to the actual eccentricities of Area X. For example, the secret knowledge that there had been a proto–Area X, a kind of *preamble* and beachhead established first. As much as seeing the mound of journals had radically altered my view of Area X, I did not think that the higher number of expeditions told me much more about the Tower and its effects. It told me primarily that even if the border was expanding, the progress of assimilation by Area X could still be considered conservative. The recurring data points found in the journals that related to repeating cycles and fluctuations of seasons of the strange and the ordinary were useful in establishing trends. But this information, too, my superiors probably knew and therefore it could be considered something already reported by others. The myth that only a few early expeditions, the start date artificially *suggested* by the Southern Reach, had come to grief reinforced the idea of cycles existing within the overall framework of an *advance*.

The individual details chronicled by the journals might tell stories of heroism or cowardice, of good decisions and bad decisions, but ultimately they spoke to a kind of *inevitability*. No one had as yet plumbed the depths of *intent* or *purpose* in a way that had obstructed that intent or purpose. Everyone had died or been killed, returned changed or returned unchanged, but Area X had continued on as it always had . . . while our superiors seemed to fear any radical reimagining of this situation so much that they had continued to send in knowledge-strapped expeditions as if this was the only option. *Feed Area X but do not antagonize it, and perhaps someone will, through luck or mere repetition, hit upon some explanation, some solution, before the world* becomes Area X.

There was no way I could corroborate any of these theories, but I took a grim comfort in coming up with them anyway.

I left my husband's journal until last, even though its pull was as strong as the allure of the Tower. Instead, I focused on what I had brought back: the samples from the ruined village and from the psychologist, along with samples of my own skin. I set up my microscope on the rickety table, which I suppose the surveyor had found already so damaged it did not require her further attention. The cells of the psychologist, both from her unaffected shoulder and her wound, appeared to be normal human cells. So did the cells I examined from my own sample. This was impossible. I checked the samples over and over, even childishly pretending I had no interest in looking at them before swooping down with an eagle eye.

I was convinced that when I wasn't looking at them, these cells became something else, that the very act of observation changed everything. I knew this was madness and yet still I thought it. I felt as if Area X were laughing at me then—every blade of grass, every stray insect, every drop of water. What would happen when the Crawler reached the bottom of the Tower? What would happen when it came back up?

Then I examined the samples from the village: moss from the "forehead" of one of the eruptions, splinters of wood, a dead fox, a rat. The wood was indeed wood. The rat was indeed a rat. The moss and the fox . . . were composed of modified human cells. *Where lies the strangling fruit that came from the hand of the sinner I shall bring forth the seeds of the dead . . .*

I suppose I should have reared back from the microscope in shock, but I was beyond such reactions to anything that instrument might show me. Instead, I contented myself with quiet cursing. The boar on the way to base camp, the strange dolphins, the tormented beast in the reeds. Even the idea that replicas of members of the eleventh expedition had crossed back over. All supported the evidence of my microscope. Transformations were taking place here, and as much as I had felt part of a "natural" landscape on my trek to the lighthouse, I could not deny that these habitats were transitional in a deeply *unnatural* way. A perverse sense of relief overtook me; at least now I had proof of something strange happening, along with the brain tissue the anthropologist had taken from the skin of the Crawler.

By then, though, I'd had enough of samples. I ate lunch and decided against putting more effort into cleaning up the camp; most of that task would have to fall to the next expedition. It was another brilliant, blinding afternoon of stunning blue sky allied with a comfortable heat. I sat for a time, watched the dragonflies skimming the long grass, the dipping, looping flight of a redheaded woodpecker. I was just putting off the inevitable, my return to the Tower, and yet still I wasted time.

When I finally picked up my husband's journal and started to read, the brightness washed over me in unending waves and connected me to the earth, the water, the trees, the air, as I opened up and kept on opening.

Nothing about my husband's journal was expected. Except for some terse, hastily scribbled exceptions, he had addressed most of the entries to me. I did not want this, and as soon as it became apparent I had to resist the need to throw the journal away from me as if it were poison. My reaction had nothing to do with love or lack of love but was more out of a sense of guilt. He had meant to share this journal with me, and now he was either truly dead or existed in a state beyond any possible way for me to communicate with him, to reciprocate.

The eleventh expedition had consisted of eight members, all male: a psychologist, two medics (including my husband), a linguist, a surveyor, a biologist, an anthropologist, and an archaeologist. They had come to Area X in the winter, when the trees had lost most of their leaves and the reeds had turned darker and thicker. The flowering bushes "became sullen" and seemed to "huddle" along the path, as he put it. "Fewer birds than indicated in reports," he wrote. "But where do they go? Only the ghost bird knows." The sky frequently clouded over, and the water level in the cypress swamps was low. "No rain the entire time we've been here," he wrote at the end of the first week.

They, too, discovered what only I call the Tower on their fifth or sixth day—I was ever more certain that the location of the base camp had been chosen to trigger that discovery—but their surveyor's opinion that they must continue mapping the wider area meant they followed a different course than ours. "None of us were eager to climb down in there," my husband wrote. "Me least of all." My husband had claustrophobia, sometimes even had to leave our bed in the middle of the night to go sleep on the deck.

For whatever reason, the psychologist did not in this case coerce the expedition to go down into the Tower. They explored farther, past the ruined village, to the lighthouse and beyond. Of the lighthouse, my husband noted their horror at discovering the signs of carnage, but of being "too respectful of the dead to put things right," by which I suppose he meant the overturned tables on the ground level. He did not mention the photograph of the lighthouse keeper on the wall of the landing, which disappointed me.

Like me, they had discovered the pile of journals at the top of the lighthouse, been shaken by it. "We had an intense argument about what to do. I wanted to abort the mission and return home because clearly we had been lied to." But it was at this point that the psychologist apparently reestablished control, if of a tenuous sort. One of the directives for Area X was for each expedition to remain a unit. But in the very next entry the expedition had decided to split up, as if to salvage the mission by catering solely to each person's will, and thus ensuring that no one would try to return to the border. The other medic, the anthropologist, the archaeologist, and the psychologist stayed in the lighthouse to read the journals and investigate the area around the lighthouse. The linguist and the biologist went back to explore the Tower. My husband and the surveyor continued on past the lighthouse.

"You would love it here," he wrote in a particularly manic entry that suggested to me not so much optimism as an unsettling euphoria. "You would love the light on the dunes. You would love the sheer expansive wildness of it."

They wandered up the coast for an entire week, mapping the landscape and fully expecting at some point to encounter the border, whatever form it might take—some obstacle that barred their progress.

But they never did.

Instead, the same habitat confronted them day after day. "We're heading north, I believe," he wrote, "but even though we cover a good fifteen to twenty miles by nightfall, nothing has changed. It is all the same," although he also was quite emphatic that he did not mean they were somehow "caught in a strange recurring loop." Yet he knew that "by all rights, we should have encountered the border by now." Indeed, they were well into an expanse of what he called the Southern Reach that had *not yet been charted*, "that we had been encouraged by the vagueness of our superiors to assume existed back beyond the border."

I, too, knew that Area X ended abruptly not far past the lighthouse. How did I know this? Our superiors had told us during training. So, in fact, I knew nothing at all.

They turned back finally because "behind us we saw strange cascading lights far distant and, from the interior, more lights, and sounds that we could not identify. We became concerned for the expedition members we had left behind." At the point when they turned back, they had come within sight of "a rocky island, the first island we have seen," which they "felt a powerful urge to explore, although there was no easy way to get over to it." The island "appeared to have been inhabited at one time—we saw stone houses dotting a hill, and a dock below."

The return trip to the lighthouse took four days, not seven, "as if the land had contracted." At the lighthouse, they found the psychologist gone and the bloody aftermath of a shoot-out on the landing halfway up. A dying survivor, the archaeologist, "told us that something 'not of the world' had come up the stairs and that it had killed the psychologist and then withdrawn with his body. 'But the psychologist came back later,' the archaeologist raved. There were only two bodies, and neither was the psychologist. He could not account for the absence. He also could not tell us why then they had shot each other, except to say 'we did not trust ourselves' over and over again." My husband noted that "some of the wounds I saw were not from bullets, and even the blood spatter on the walls did not correspond to what I knew of crime scenes. There was a strange residue on the floor."

The archaeologist "propped himself up in the corner of the landing and threatened to shoot us if I came close enough to see to his wounds. Soon enough, though, he was dead." Afterward, they dragged the bodies from the landing and buried them high up on the beach a little distance from the lighthouse. "It was difficult, ghost bird, and I don't know that we ever really recovered. Not really."

This left the linguist and the biologist at the Tower. "The surveyor suggested either going back up the coast past the lighthouse or following the beach down the coast. But we both knew this was just an avoidance of the facts. What he was really saying was that we should abandon the mission, that we should lose ourselves in the landscape."

That landscape was impinging on them now. The temperature dipped and rose violently. There were rumblings deep underground that manifested as slight tremors. The sun came to them with a "greenish tinge" as if "somehow the border were distorting our vision." They also "saw flocks of birds headed inland—not of the same species, but hawks and ducks, herons and eagles all grouped together as if in common cause."

At the Tower, they ventured only a few levels down before coming back up. I noticed no mention of words on the wall. "If the linguist and the biologist were inside, they were much farther down, but we had no interest in following them." They returned to base camp, only to find the body of the biologist, stabbed several times. The linguist had left a note that read simply, "Went to the tunnel. Do not look for me." I felt a strange pang of sympathy for a fallen colleague. No doubt the biologist had tried to reason with the linguist. Or so I told myself. Perhaps he had tried to kill the linguist. But the linguist had clearly already been ensnared by the Tower, by the words of the Crawler. Knowing the meaning of the words on such intimate terms might have been too much for anyone, I realize now.

The surveyor and my husband returned to the Tower at dusk. Why is not apparent from the journal entries—there began to be breaks that corresponded to the passage of some hours, with no recap. But during the night, they saw a ghastly procession heading into the Tower: seven of the eight members of the eleventh expedition, including a doppelgänger of my husband and the surveyor. "And there before me, *myself*. I walked so stiffly. I had such a blank look on my face. It was so clearly not me . . . and yet it was me. A kind of shock froze both me and the surveyor. We did not try to stop them. Somehow, it seemed impossible to try to stop *ourselves*—and I won't lie, we were terrified. We could do nothing but watch until they had descended. For a moment afterward, it all made sense to me, everything that had happened. We were dead. We were ghosts roaming a haunted landscape, and although we didn't know it, people lived normal lives here, everything was as it should be here . . . but we couldn't see it through the veil, the interference."

Slowly my husband shook off this feeling. They waited hidden in the trees beyond the Tower for several hours, to see if the doppelgängers would return. They argued about what they would do if that happened. The surveyor wanted to kill them. My husband wanted to interrogate them. In their residual shock, neither of them made much of the fact that the psychologist was not among their number. At one point, a sound like hissing steam emanated from the Tower and a beam of light shot out into the sky, then abruptly cut off. But still no one emerged, and eventually the two men returned to base camp.

It was at this point that they decided to go their separate ways. The surveyor had seen all he cared to see and planned to return down the trail from base camp to the border immediately. My husband refused because he suspected from some of the readings in the journal that "this idea of return through the same means as our entry might in fact be a trap." My husband had, over the course of time, having encountered no obstacle to travel farther north, "grown suspicious of the entire idea of borders," although he could not yet synthesize "the intensity of this feeling" into a coherent theory.

Interspersed with this direct account of what had happened to the expedition were more personal observations, most of which I am reluctant to summarize here. Except there is one passage that pertains to Area X and to our relationship, too:

Seeing all of this, experiencing all of it, even when it's bad, I wish you were here. I wish we had volunteered together. I would have understood you better here, on the trek north. We wouldn't have needed to say anything if you didn't want to. It wouldn't have bothered me. Not at all. And we wouldn't have turned back. We would have kept going until we couldn't go farther.

Slowly, painfully, I realized what I had been reading from the very first words of his journal. My husband had had an inner life that went beyond his gregarious exterior, and if I had known enough to let him inside my guard, I might have understood this fact. Except I hadn't, of course. I had let tidal pools and fungi that could devour plastic inside my guard, but not him. Of all the aspects of the journal, this ate at me the most. He had created his share of our problems—by pushing me too hard, by wanting too much, by trying to see something in me that didn't exist. But I could have met him partway and retained my sovereignty. And now it was too late.

His personal observations included many grace notes. A description in the margin of a tidal pool in the rocks down the coast just beyond the lighthouse. A lengthy observation of the atypical use of an outcropping of oysters at low tide by a skimmer seeking to kill a large fish. Photographs of the tidal pool had been stuck in a sleeve in the back. Placed carefully in the sleeve, too, were pressed wildflowers, a slender seedpod, a few unusual leaves. My husband would have cared little for any of this; even the focus to observe the skimmer and write a page of notes would have required great concentration from him. I knew these elements were intended for me and me alone. There were no endearments, but I understood in part because of this restraint. He knew how much I hated words like *love*.

The last entry, written upon his return to the lighthouse, read, "I am going back up the coast. But not on foot. There was a boat in the ruined village. Staved in, rotting, but I have enough wood from the wall outside the lighthouse to fix it. I'll follow the shoreline as far as I can go. To the island, and perhaps beyond. If you ever read this, that is where I am going. That is where I will be." Could there be, even within all of these transitional ecosystems, one still more transitional—at the limits of the Tower's influence but not yet under the border's influence?

After reading the journal, I was left with the comfort of that essential recurring image of my husband putting out to sea in a boat he had rebuilt, out through the crashing surf to the calm just beyond. Of him following the coastline north, alone, seeking in that experience the joy of small moments remembered from happier days. It made me fiercely proud of him. It showed resolve. It showed bravery. It bound him to me in a more intimate way than we had ever seemed to have while together.

In glimmers, in shreds of thought, in the aftermath of my reading, I wondered if he kept a journal still, or if the dolphin's eye had been familiar for a reason other than that it was so human. But soon enough I banished this nonsense; some questions will ruin you if you are denied the answer long enough.

My injuries had receded into a constant but manageable ache when I breathed. Not coincidentally, by nightfall, the brightness was thrushing up through my lungs and into my throat again so that I imagined wisps of it misting from my mouth. I shuddered at the thought of the psychologist's plume, seen from afar, like a distress signal. I couldn't wait for morning, even if this was just a premonition of a far-distant future. I would return to the Tower *now*. It was the only place for me to go. I left behind the assault rifle and all but one gun. I left my knife. I left my knapsack, affixed a water canteen to my belt. I took my camera, but then thought better of it and abandoned it by a rock halfway to the Tower. It would just distract, this impulse to record, and photographs mattered no more than samples. I had decades of journals waiting for me in the lighthouse. I had generations of expeditions that had ghosted on ahead of me. The pointlessness of that, the pressure of that, almost got to me again. The waste of it all.

I had brought a flashlight but found I could see well enough by the green glow that emanated from my own body. I crept quickly through the dark, along the path leading to the Tower. The black sky, free of clouds, framed by the tall narrow lines formed by pine trees, reflected the full immensity of the heavens. No borders, no artificial light to obscure the thousands of glinting pinpricks. I could see everything. As a child, I had stared up at the night sky and searched for shooting stars like everyone else. As an adult, sitting on the roof of my cottage near the bay, and later, haunting the empty lot, I looked not for shooting stars but for fixed ones, and I would try to imagine what kind of life lived in those celestial tidal pools so far from us. The stars I saw now looked strange, strewn across the dark in chaotic new patterns, where just the night before I had taken comfort in their familiarity. Was I only now seeing them clearly? Was I perhaps even farther from home than I had thought? There shouldn't have been a grim sort of satisfaction in the thought.

The heartbeat came to me more distantly as I entered the Tower, my mask tied tightly in place over my nose and mouth. I did not know if I was keeping further contamination out or just trying to contain my brightness. The bioluminescence of the words on the wall had intensified, and the glow from my exposed skin seemed to respond in kind, lighting my way. Otherwise, I sensed no difference as I descended past the first levels. If these upper reaches had become familiar that feeling was balanced by the sobering fact that this was my first time alone in the Tower. With each new curve of those walls down into further darkness, dispelled only by the grainy, green light, I came more and more to expect something to erupt out of the shadows to attack me. I missed the surveyor in those moments and had to tamp down my guilt. And, despite my concentration, I found I was drawn to the words on the wall, that even as I tried to concentrate on the greater depths, those words kept bringing me back. *There shall be in the planting in the shadows a grace and a mercy that shall bloom dark flowers, and their teeth shall devour and sustain and herald the passing of an age . . .*

Sooner than expected, I came to the place where we had found the anthropologist dead. Somehow it surprised me that she still lay there, surrounded by the debris of her passage—scraps of cloth, her empty knapsack, a couple of broken vials, her head forming a broken outline. She was covered with a moving carpet of pale organisms that, as I stooped close, I discovered were the tiny hand-shaped parasites that lived among the words on the wall. It was impossible to tell if they were protecting her, changing her, or breaking her body down—just as I could not know whether some version of the anthropologist had indeed appeared to the surveyor near base camp after I had left for the lighthouse . . .

I did not linger but continued farther down.

Now the Tower's heartbeat began to echo and become louder. Now the words on the wall once again became fresher, as if only just "dried" after creation. I became aware of a hum under the heartbeat, almost a staticky buzzing sound. The brittle mustiness of that space ceded to something more tropical and cloying. I found that I was sweating. Most important, the track of the Crawler beneath my boots became fresher, stickier, and I tried to favor the right-hand wall to avoid the substance. That right-hand wall had changed, too, in that a thin layer of moss or lichen covered it. I did not like having to press my back up against it to avoid the substance on the floor, but I had no choice.

After about two hours of slowed progress, the heartbeat of the Tower had risen to a point where it seemed to shake the stairs, and the underlying hum splintered into a fresh crackling. My ears rang with it, my body vibrated with it, and I was sweating through my clothes due to the humidity, the stuffiness almost making me want to take off my mask in an attempt to gulp down air. But I resisted the temptation. I was close. I knew I was close . . . to what, I had no idea.

The words on the wall here were so freshly formed that they appeared to drip, and the hand-shaped creatures were less numerous, and those that did manifest formed closed fists, as if not yet quite awake and alive. *That which dies shall still know life in death for all that decays is not forgotten and reanimated shall walk the world in a bliss of not-knowing . . .*

I spiraled around one more set of stairs, and then as I came into the narrow straightaway before the next curve . . . I saw *light*. The edges of a sharp, golden light that emanated from a place beyond my vision, hidden by the wall, and the brightness within me throbbed and thrilled to it. The buzzing sound again intensified until it was so jagged and hissing that I felt as if blood might trickle from my ears. The heartbeat overtop boomed into every part of me. I did not feel as if I were a person but simply a receiving station for a series of overwhelming transmissions. I could feel the brightness spewing from my mouth in a half-invisible spray, meeting the resistance of the mask, and I tore it off with a gasp. *Give back to that which gave to you*, came the thought, not knowing what I might be feeding, or what it meant for the collection of cells and thoughts that comprised me.

You understand, I could no more have turned back than have gone back in time. My free will was compromised, if only by the severe temptation of the unknown. To have quit that place, to have returned to the surface, without rounding that corner . . . my imagination would have tormented me forever. In that moment, I had convinced myself I would rather die knowing . . . something, *anything*.

I passed the threshold. I descended into the light.

One night during the last months at Rock Bay I found myself intensely restless. This was after I had confirmed that my grant wouldn't be renewed and before I had any prospects of a new job. I had brought another stranger I knew back from the bar to try to distract myself from my situation, but he had left hours ago. I had a wakefulness that I could not shake, and I was still drunk. It was stupid and dangerous, but I decided to get in my truck and drive out to the tidal pools. I wanted to creep up on all of that hidden life and try to surprise it somehow. I had gotten it into my mind that the tidal pools changed during the night when no one watched. This is what happens, perhaps, if you have been studying something so long that you can tell one sea anemone from another in an instant, could have picked out any denizen of those tidal pools from a lineup if it had committed a crime.

So I parked the truck, took the winding trail down to the grainy beach, making my way with the aid of a tiny flashlight attached to my key chain. Then I sloshed through the shallows and climbed up onto the sheet of rock. I really wanted to lose myself. People my entire life have told me I am too much in control, but that has never been the case. I have never truly been in control, have never wanted control.

That night, even though I had come up with a thousand excuses to blame others, I knew I had screwed up. Not filing reports. Not sticking to the focus of the job. Recording odd data from the periphery. Nothing that might satisfy the organization that had provided the grant. I was the queen of the tidal pools, and what I said was the law, and what I reported was what I had wanted to report. I had gotten sidetracked, like I always did, because I melted into my surroundings, could not remain *separate from*, *apart from*, objectivity a foreign land to me.

I went to tidal pool after tidal pool with my pathetic

flashlight, losing my balance half a dozen times and almost falling. If anyone had been observing—and who is to say now that they were not?—they would have seen a cursing, half-drunk, reckless biologist who had lost all perspective, who was out in the middle of nowhere for the second straight year and feeling vulnerable and lonely, even though she'd promised herself she would never get lonely. *The things she had done and said that society labeled antisocial or selfish.* Seeking something in the tidal pools that night even though what she found during the day was miraculous enough. She might even have been shouting, screaming, whirling about on those slippery rocks as if the best boots in the world couldn't fail you, send you falling to crack your skull, give you a forehead full of limpets and barnacles and blood.

But the fact is, even though I didn't deserve it—did I deserve it? and had I really just been looking for something familiar?—I found something miraculous, something that uncovered itself with its own light. I spied a glinting, wavery promise of illumination coming from one of the larger tidal pools, and it gave me pause. Did I really want a sign? Did I really want to discover something or did I just think I did? Well, I decided I did want to discover something, because I walked toward it, suddenly sobered up enough to watch my steps, to shuffle along so I wouldn't crack my skull before I saw whatever it was in that pool.

What I found when I finally stood there, hands on bent knees, peering down into that tidal pool, was a rare species of colossal starfish, six-armed, larger than a saucepan, that bled a dark gold color into the still water as if it were on fire. Most of us professionals eschewed its scientific name for the more apt "destroyer of worlds." It was covered in thick spines, and along the edges I could just see, fringed with emerald green, the most delicate of transparent cilia, thousands of them, propelling it along upon its appointed route as it searched for its prey: other, lesser starfish. I had never seen a destroyer of worlds before, even in an aquarium, and it was so unexpected that I forgot about the slippery rock and, shifting my balance, almost fell, steadying myself with one arm propped against the edge of the tidal pool.

But the longer I stared at it, the less comprehensible the creature became. The more it became something alien to me, and the more I had a sense that I knew nothing at all—about nature, about ecosystems. There was something about my mood and its dark glow that eclipsed sense, that made me see this creature, which had indeed been assigned a place in the taxonomy—catalogued, studied, and described—irreducible down to any of that. And if I kept looking, I knew that ultimately I would have to admit I knew less than nothing about myself as well, whether that was a lie or the truth.

When I finally wrenched my gaze from the starfish and stood again, I could not tell where the sky met the sea, whether I faced the water or the shore. I was completely adrift, and dislocated, and all I had to navigate by in that moment was the glowing beacon below me.

Turning that corner, encountering the Crawler for the first time, was a similar experience at a thousand times the magnitude. If on those rocks those many years ago I could not tell sea from shore, here I could not tell stairs from ceiling, and even though I steadied myself with an arm against the wall, the wall seemed to cave in before my touch, and I struggled to keep from falling through it.

There, in the depths of the Tower, I could not begin to

understand what I was looking at and even now I have to work hard to pull it together from fragments. It is difficult to tell what blanks my mind might be filling in just to remove the weight of so many unknowns.

Did I say I had seen golden light? As soon as I turned that corner entire, it was no longer golden but blue-green, and the blue-green light was like nothing I had experienced before. It surged out, blinding and bleeding and thick and layered and absorbing. It so overwhelmed my ability to comprehend shapes within it that I forced myself to switch from sight, to focus at first on reports from other senses.

The sound that came to me now was like a crescendo of ice or ice crystals shattering to form an unearthly noise that I had mistaken earlier for buzzing, and which began to take on an intense melody and rhythm that filled my brain. Vaguely, from some far-off place, I realized that the words on the wall were being infused with sound as well, but that I had not had the capacity to hear it before. The vibration had a texture and a weight, and with it came a burning smell, as of late fall leaves or like some vast and distant engine close to overheating. The taste on my tongue was like brine set ablaze.

No words can . . . no photographs could . . .

As I adjusted to the light, the Crawler kept changing at a lightning pace, as if to mock my ability to comprehend it. It was a figure within a series of refracted panes of glass. It was a series of layers in the shape of an archway. It was a great sluglike monster ringed by satellites of even odder creatures. It was a glistening star. My eyes kept glancing off of it as if an optic nerve was not enough.

Then it became an overwhelming *hugeness* in my

battered vision, seeming to rise and keep rising as it leapt toward me. The shape spread until it was even where it was not, or *should not have been*. It seemed now more like a kind of obstacle or wall or thick closed door blocking the stairs. Not a wall of light—gold, blue, green, existing in some other spectrum—but a wall of flesh that *resembled* light, with sharp, curving elements within it and textures like ice when it has frozen from flowing water. An impression of living things lazily floating in the air around it like soft tadpoles, but at the limits of my vision so I could not tell if this was akin to those floating dark motes that are tricks of the eye, that do not exist.

Within this fractured mass, within all of these different impressions of the Crawler—half-blinded but still triangulating through my other senses—I thought I saw a darker shadow of an arm or a kind of *echo* of an arm in constant blurring motion, continuously imparting to the left-hand wall a repetition of depth and signal that made its progress laboriously slow—its message, its code of change, of recalibrations and adjustments, of transformations. And, perhaps, another dark shadow, vaguely head-shaped, above the arm—but as indistinct as if I had been swimming in murky water and seen in the distance a shape obscured by thick seaweed.

I tried to pull back now, to creep back up the steps. But I couldn't. Whether because the Crawler had trapped me or my brain had betrayed me, I could not move.

The Crawler changed or I was beginning to black out repeatedly and come back to consciousness. It would appear as if nothing was there, nothing at all, as if the words wrote themselves, and then the Crawler would tremble into being and then wink out again, and all that remained constant was a suggestion of an arm and the impression of the words being written.

What can you do when your five senses are not enough? Because I still couldn't truly *see* it here, any more than I had seen it under the microscope, and that's what scared me the most. Why couldn't I *see* it? In my mind, I stood over the starfish at Rock Bay, and the starfish grew and grew until it was not just the tidal pool but the world, and I was teetering on its rough, luminous surface, staring up at the night sky again, while the light of it flowed up and through me.

Against the awful pressure of that light, as if the entire weight of Area X were concentrated here, I changed tactics, tried to focus just on the creation of the words on the wall, the impression of a head or a helmet or . . . what? . . . somewhere above the arm. A cascade of sparks that I knew were living organisms. A new word upon the wall. And me still not seeing, and the brightness coiled within me assumed an almost hushed quality, as if we were in a cathedral.

The enormity of this experience combined with the heartbeat and the crescendo of sound from its ceaseless writing to fill me up until I had no room left. *This* moment, which I might have been waiting for my entire life all unknowing— this moment of an encounter with the most beautiful, the most terrible thing I might ever experience—was beyond me. What inadequate recording equipment I had brought with me and what an inadequate name I had chosen for it—the Crawler. Time elongated, was nothing but fuel for the words this thing had created on the wall for who knew how many years for who knew what purpose.

I don't know how long I stood at the threshold, watching

the Crawler, frozen. I might have watched it forever and never noticed the awful passage of the years.

But then what?

What occurs after revelation and paralysis?

Either death or a slow and certain thawing. A returning to the physical world. It is not that I became used to the Crawler's presence but that I reached a point—a single infinitesimal moment—when I once again recognized that the Crawler was an organism. A complex, unique, intricate, awe-inspiring, dangerous organism. It might be inexplicable. It might be beyond the limits of my senses to capture—or my science or my intellect—but I still believed I was in the presence of some kind of living creature, one that practiced mimicry using my own thoughts. For even then, I believed that it might be pulling these different impressions of itself from my mind and projecting them back at me, as a form of camouflage. To thwart the biologist in me, to frustrate the logic left in me.

With an effort I could feel in the groan of my limbs, a dislocation in my bones, I managed to turn my back on the Crawler.

Just that simple, wrenching act was such a relief, as I hugged the far wall in all its cool roughness. I closed my eyes—why did I need vision when all it did was keep betraying me?—and started to crab-walk my way back, still feeling the light upon my back. Feeling the music from the words. The gun I had forgotten all about digging into my hip. The very idea of *gun* now seemed as pathetic and useless as the word *sample*. Both implied aiming at something. What was there to aim at?

I had only made it a step or two when I felt a rising sense of heat and weight and a kind of licking, lapping wetness, as if the thick light was transforming into the sea itself. I had thought perhaps I was about to escape, but it wasn't true. With just one more step away, as I began to choke, I realized that the light *had* become a sea.

Somehow, even though I was not truly underwater, I was drowning.

The franticness that rose within me was the awful formless panic of a child who had fallen into a fountain and known, for the first time, as her lungs filled with water, that she could die. There was no end to it, no way to get past it. I was awash in a brothy green-blue ocean alight with sparks. And I just kept on drowning and struggling against the drowning, until some part of me realized I would keep drowning forever. I imagined tumbling from the rocks, falling, battered by the surf. Washing up thousands of miles from where I was, unrecognizable, in some other form, but still retaining the awful memory of this moment.

Then I felt the impression from behind me of hundreds of eyes beginning to turn in my direction, staring at me. I was a thing in a swimming pool being observed by a monstrous little girl. I was a mouse in an empty lot being tracked by a fox. I was the prey the starfish had reached up and pulled down into the tidal pool.

In some watertight compartment, the brightness told me I had to accept that I would not survive that moment. I wanted to live—I really did. But I couldn't any longer. I couldn't even breathe any longer. So I opened my mouth and welcomed the water, welcomed the torrent. Except it wasn't really water. And the eyes upon me were not eyes, and I was pinned there now by the Crawler, had let it in, I realized, so that its full regard was upon me and I could not move, could not think, was helpless and alone.

A raging waterfall crashed down on my mind, but the water was comprised of fingers, a hundred fingers, probing and pressing down into the skin of my neck, and then punching up through the bone of the back of my skull and into my brain . . . and then the pressure eased even though the impression of unlimited force did not let up and for a time, still drowning, an icy calm came over me, and through the calm bled a kind of monumental blue-green light. I smelled a burning inside my own head and there came a moment when I screamed, my skull crushed to dust and reassembled, mote by mote.

There shall be a fire that knows your name, and in the presence of the strangling fruit, its dark flame shall acquire every part of you.

It was the most agony I have ever been in, as if a metal rod had been repeatedly thrust into me and then the pain distributed like a second skin inside the contours of my outline. Everything became tinged with the red. I blacked out. I came to. I blacked out, came to, blacked out, still perpetually gasping for breath, knees buckling, scrabbling at the wall for support. My mouth opened so wide from the shrieking that something popped in my jaw. I think I stopped breathing for a minute but the brightness inside experienced no such interruption. It just kept oxygenating my blood.

Then the terrible invasiveness was gone, ripped away, and with it the sensation of drowning and the thick sea that had surrounded me. There came a *push*, and the Crawler tossed me aside, down the steps beyond it. I washed up there, bruised and crumpled. With nothing to lean against, I fell like a sack, crumbling before something that was never meant to be, something never meant to invade me. I sucked in air in great shuddering gasps.

But I couldn't stay there, still within the range of its regard. I had no choice now. Throat raw, my insides feeling eviscerated, I flung myself down into the greater dark below the Crawler, on my hands and knees at first, scrabbling to escape, taken over by a blind, panicked impulse to get out of the sight of it.

Only when the light behind me had faded, only when I felt safe, did I drop to the floor again. I lay there for a long time. Apparently, I was recognizable to the Crawler now. Apparently, I was words it could understand, unlike the anthropologist. I wondered if my cells would long be able to hide their transformation from me. I wondered if this was the beginning of the end. But mostly I felt the utter relief of having passed a gauntlet, if barely. The brightness deep within was curled up, traumatized.

Perhaps my only real expertise, my only talent, is to endure beyond the endurable. I don't know when I managed to stand again, to continue on, legs rubbery. I don't know how long that took, but eventually I got up.

Soon the spiral stairs straightened out, and with this straightening, the stifling humidity abruptly lessened and the tiny creatures that lived on the wall were no longer to be seen, and the sounds from the Crawler above took on a more muffled texture. Though I still saw the ghosts of past scrawlings on the wall, even my own luminescence became muted here. I was wary of that tracery of words, as if some- how they could hurt me as surely as the Crawler, and yet there was some comfort in following them. Here the varia- tions were more legible and now made more sense to me. *And it came for me. And it cast out all else.* Retraced again and again. Were the words more naked down here, or did I just possess more knowledge now?

I couldn't help but notice that these new steps shared the depth and width of the lighthouse steps almost exactly. Above me, the unbroken surface of the ceiling had changed so that now a profusion of deep, curving grooves criss- crossed it.

I stopped to drink water. I stopped to catch my breath. The aftershock of the encounter with the Crawler was still washing over me in waves. When I continued, it was with a kind of numbed awareness that there might be more revela- tions still to absorb, that I had to prepare myself. Somehow.

A few minutes later, a tiny rectangular block of fuzzy white light began to take form, shape, far below. As I de- scended, it became larger with a reluctance I can only call hesitation. After another half hour, I thought it must be a kind of door, but the haziness remained, almost as if it were obscuring itself.

The closer I got, and with it still distant, the more I was also certain that this door bore an uncanny resemblance to the door I had seen in my glance back after having crossed the border on our way to base camp. The very vagueness of it triggered this response because it was a specific kind of vagueness.

In the next half hour after that, I began to feel an in- stinctual urge to turn back, which I overrode by telling myself I could not yet face the return journey and the Crawler again. But the grooves in the ceiling hurt to look at, as if they ran across the outside of my own skull, continually being remade there. They had become lines of some repelling force. An hour later, as that shimmering white rectangle became larger but no more distinct, I was filled with such a feeling of *wrongness* that I suffered nausea. The idea of a *trap* grew in my mind, that this floating light in the darkness was not a door at all but the maw of some beast, and if I entered through it to the other side, it would devour me.

Finally I came to a halt. The words continued, unrelenting, downward, and I estimated the door lay no more than another five or six hundred steps below me. It blazed in my vision now; I could feel a rawness to my skin as if I were getting a sunburn from looking at it. I wanted to continue on, but I could not continue on. I could not will my legs to do it, could not force my mind to overcome the fear and uneasiness. Even the temporary absence of the brightness, as if hiding, counseled against further progress.

I remained there, sitting on the steps, watching the door, for some time. I worried that this sensation was residual hypnotic compulsion, that even from beyond death the psychologist had found a way to manipulate me. Perhaps there had been some encoded order or directive my infection had not been able to circumvent or override. Was I in the end stages of some prolonged form of annihilation?

The reason didn't matter, though. I knew I would never reach the door. I would become so sick I wouldn't be able to move, and I would never make it back to the surface, eyes cut and blinded by the grooves in the ceiling. I would be stuck on the steps, just like the anthropologist, and almost as much of a failure as she and the psychologist had been at recognizing the impossible. So I turned around, and, in a great deal of pain, feeling as if I had left part of myself there, I began to trudge back up those steps, the image of a hazy door of light as large in my imagination as the immensity of the Crawler.

I remember the sensation in that moment of turning away that something was now peering out at me from the door below, but when I glanced over my shoulder, only the familiar hazy white brilliance greeted me.

I wish I could say that the rest of the journey was a blur, as if I were indeed the flame the psychologist had seen, and I was staring out through my own burning. I wish that what came next was sunlight and the surface. But, although I had earned the right for it to be over . . . it was not over.

I remember every painful, scary step back up, every moment of it. I remember halting before I turned the corner where again lay the Crawler, still busy and incomprehensible in its task. Unsure if I could endure the excavation of my mind once more. Unsure if I would go mad from the sensation of drowning this time, no matter how much reason told me it was an illusion. But also knowing that the weaker I became, the more my mind would betray me. Soon it would be easy to retreat into the shadows, to become some *shell* haunting the lower steps. I might never have more strength or resolve to summon than in that moment.

I let go of Rock Bay, of the starfish in its pool. I thought instead about my husband's journal. I thought about my husband, in a boat, somewhere to the north. I thought about how everything lay above, and nothing now below.

So, I hugged the wall again. So, I closed my eyes again.

So, I endured the light again, and flinched and moaned, expecting the rush of the sea into my mouth, and my head cracked open . . . but none of that happened. None of it, and I don't know why, except that having scanned and sampled me, and having, based on some unknown criteria, released me once, the Crawler no longer displayed any interest in me.

I was almost out of sight above it, rounding the corner, when some stubborn part of me insisted on risking a single glance back. One last ill-advised, defiant glance at something I might never understand.

Staring back at me amid that profusion of selves generated by the Crawler, I saw, barely visible, the face of a man, hooded in shadow and orbited by indescribable things I could think of only as his jailers.

The man's expression displayed such a complex and naked extremity of emotion that it transfixed me. I saw on those features the endurance of an unending pain and sorrow, yes, but shining through as well a kind of grim satisfaction and *ecstasy*. I had never seen such an expression before, but I recognized that face. I had seen it in a photograph. A *sharp, eagle's eye gleamed out from a heavy face, the left eye lost to his squint. A thick beard hid all but a hint of a firm chin under it.*

Trapped within the Crawler, the last lighthouse keeper stared out at me, so it seemed, not just across a vast, un-bridgeable gulf but also out across the years. For, though thinner—his eyes receded in their orbits, his jawline more pronounced—the lighthouse keeper had not aged a day since that photograph was taken more than thirty years ago. This man who now existed in a place none of us could comprehend.

Did he know what he had become or had he gone mad long ago? Could he even really see me?

I do not know how long he had been looking at me, observing me, before I had turned to see him. Or if he had even existed before I saw him. But he was real to me, even though I held his gaze for such a short time, too short a time, and I cannot say anything passed between us. How long would have been enough? There was *nothing* I could do for him, and I had no room left in me for anything but my own survival.

There might be far worse things than drowning. I could not tell what he had lost, or what he might have gained, over the past thirty years, but I envied him that journey not at all.

I never dreamed before Area X, or at least I never remembered my dreams. My husband found this strange and told me once that maybe this meant I lived in a continuous dream from which I had never woken up. Perhaps he meant it as a joke, perhaps not. He had, after all, been haunted by a nightmare for years, had been shaped by it, until it had all fallen away from him, revealed as a facade. A *house and a basement and the awful crimes that had occurred there*.

But I'd had an exhausting day at work and took it seriously. Especially because it was the last week before he left on the expedition.

"We all live in a kind of continuous dream," I told him.

"When we wake, it is because something, some event, some pinprick even, disturbs the edges of what we've taken as reality."

"Am I a pinprick then, disturbing the edges of your reality, ghost bird?" he asked, and this time I caught the desperation of his mood.

"Oh, is it bait-the-ghost-bird time again?" I said, arching an eyebrow. I didn't feel that relaxed. I felt sick to my stomach, but it seemed important to be normal for him. When he later came back and I saw what normal could be, I wished I'd been abnormal, that I'd shouted, that I'd done anything but be banal.

"Perhaps I'm a figment of your reality," he said. "Perhaps I don't exist except to do your bidding."

"Then you're failing spectacularly," I said as I made my way into the kitchen for a glass of water. He was already on a second glass of wine.

"Or succeeding spectacularly because you want me to fail," he said, but he was smiling.

He came up behind me then to hug me. He had thick forearms and a wide chest. His hands were hopeless man-hands, like something that should live in a cave, ridiculously strong, and an asset when he went sailing. The antiseptic rubber smell of Band-Aids suffused him like a particularly unctuous cologne. He was one big Band-Aid, placed directly on the wound.

"Ghost bird, where would you be if we weren't together?" he asked.

I had no answer for that. *Not here. Not there, either. Maybe nowhere.*

Then: "Ghost bird?"

"Yes," I said, resigned to my nickname.

"Ghost bird, I'm afraid now," he said. "I'm afraid and I have a selfish thing to ask. A thing I have no right to ask."

"Ask it anyway." I was still angry, but in those last days I had become reconciled to my loss, had compartmentalized it so I would not withhold my affection from him. There was a part of me, too, that raged against the systematic loss of my field assignments, was envious of his opportunity. That gloated about the empty lot because it was mine alone.

"Will you come after me if I don't come back? If you can?"

"You're coming back," I told him. To sit right here, like a golem, with all the things I knew about you drained out.

How I wish, beyond reason, that I had answered him, even to tell him no. And how I wish now—even though it was always impossible—that, in the end, I *had* gone to Area X for him.

A *swimming pool*. A *rocky bay*. An *empty lot*. A *tower*. A *light-house*. These things are real and not real. They exist and they do not exist. I remake them in my mind with every new thought, every remembered detail, and each time they are slightly different. Sometimes they are camouflage or disguises. Sometimes they are something more truthful.

When I finally reached the surface, I lay on my back atop the Tower, too exhausted to move, smiling for the simple, unexpected pleasure of the heat on my eyelids from the morning sun. I was continually reimagining the world even then, the lighthouse keeper colonizing my thoughts. I kept pulling out the photograph from my pocket, staring at his face, as if he held some further answer I could not yet grasp.

I wanted—I needed—to know that I had indeed seen him, not some apparition conjured up by the Crawler, and I clutched at anything that would help me believe that. What convinced me the most wasn't the photograph—it was the sample the anthropologist had taken from the edge of the Crawler, the sample that had proven to be human brain tissue.

So with that as my anchor, I began to form a narrative for the lighthouse keeper, as best I could, even as I stood and once again made my way back to the base camp. It was difficult because I knew nothing at all about his life, had none of those indicators that might have allowed me to imagine him. I had just a photograph and that terrible glimpse of him inside the Tower. All I could think was that this was a man who had had a normal life once, perhaps, but not one of those familiar rituals that defined normal had had any permanence—or helped him. He had been caught up in a storm that hadn't yet abated. Perhaps he had even seen it coming from the top of the lighthouse, the Event arriving like a kind of wave.

And what had manifested? What do I believe manifested? Think of it as a thorn, perhaps, a long, thick thorn so large it is buried deep in the side of the world. Injecting itself into the world. Emanating from this giant thorn is an endless, perhaps automatic, need to assimilate and to mimic. Assimilator and assimilated interact through the catalyst of a script of words, which powers the engine of transformation. Perhaps it is a creature living in perfect symbiosis with a host of other creatures. Perhaps it is "merely" a machine. But in either instance, if it has intelligence, that intelligence is far different from our own. It creates out of our ecosystem a new world, whose processes and aims are utterly alien—one that works through supreme acts of mirroring, and by remaining hidden in so many other ways, all without surrendering the foundations of its *otherness* as it becomes what it encounters.

I do not know how this thorn got here or from how far away it came, but by luck or fate or design at some point it found the lighthouse keeper and did not let him go. How long he had as it remade him, repurposed him, is a mystery. There was no one to observe, to bear witness—until thirty years later a biologist catches a glimpse of him and speculates on what he might have become. Catalyst. Spark. Engine. The grit that made the pearl? Or merely an unwilling passenger?

And after his fate was determined . . . imagine the expeditions—twelve or fifty or a hundred, it doesn't matter—that keep coming into contact with that entity or entities, that keep becoming fodder and becoming remade. These expeditions that come here at a hidden entry point along a mysterious border, an entry point that (perhaps) is mirrored within the deepest depths of the Tower. Imagine these expeditions, and then recognize that *they all still exist* in Area X in some form, even the ones that came back, especially the ones that came back: layered over one another, communicating in whatever way is left to them. Imagine that this communication sometimes lends a sense of the uncanny to the landscape because of the narcissism of our human gaze, but that it is just part of the natural world here. I may never know what triggered the creation of the doppelgängers, but it may not matter.

Imagine, too, that while the Tower makes and remakes the world inside the border, it also slowly sends its emissaries across that border in ever greater numbers, so that in tangled gardens and fallow fields its envoys begin their work. *How does it travel and how far? What strange matter mixes and mingles?* In some future moment, perhaps the infiltration will reach even a certain remote sheet of coastal rock, quietly germinate in those tidal pools I know so well. Unless, of course, I am wrong that Area X is rousing itself from slumber, changing, becoming *different* than it was before.

The terrible thing, the thought I cannot dislodge after all I have seen, is that I can no longer say with conviction that this is a bad thing. Not when looking at the pristine nature of Area X and then the world beyond, which we have altered so much. Before she died, the psychologist said I had changed, and I think she meant I had *changed sides*. It isn't true—I don't even know if there are sides, or what that might mean—but it *could* be true. I see now that I could be persuaded. A religious or superstitious person, someone who believed in angels or in demons, might see it differently. Almost anyone else might see it differently. But I am not those people. I am just the biologist; I don't require any of this to have a deeper meaning.

I am aware that all of this speculation is incomplete, inexact, inaccurate, useless. If I don't have real answers, it is because we still don't know what questions to ask. Our instruments are useless, our methodology broken, our motivations selfish.

There is nothing much left to tell you, though I haven't quite told it right. But I am done trying anyway. After I left the Tower, I returned to base camp briefly, and then I came here, to the top of the lighthouse. I have spent four long days perfecting this account you are reading, for all its faults, and it is supplemented by a second journal that records all of my findings from the various samples taken by myself and other members of the expedition. I have even written a note for my parents.

I have bound these materials together with my husband's journal and will leave them here, atop the pile beneath the trapdoor. The table and the rug have been moved so that anyone can find what once was hidden. I also have replaced the lighthouse keeper's photograph in its frame and put it back on the wall of the landing. I have added a second circle around his face because I could not help myself.

If the hints in the journals are accurate, then when the Crawler reaches the end of its latest cycle within the Tower, Area X will enter a convulsive season of barricades and blood, a kind of cataclysmic molting, if you want to think of it that way. Perhaps even sparked by the spread of activated spores erupting from the words written by the Crawler. The past two nights, I have seen a growing cone of energy rising above the Tower and spilling out into the surrounding wilderness. Although nothing has yet come out of the sea, from the ruined village figures have emerged and headed for the Tower. From base camp, no sign of life. From the beach below, there is not even a boot left of the psychologist, as if she has melted into the sand. Every night, the moaning creature has let me know that it retains dominion over its kingdom of reeds.

Observing all of this has quelled the last ashes of the burning compulsion I had to *know everything* . . . anything . . . and in its place remains the knowledge that the brightness is not done with me. It is just beginning, and the thought of continually doing harm to myself to remain human seems somehow pathetic. I will not be here when the thirteenth expedition reaches base camp. (Have they seen me yet, or are they about to? Will I melt into this landscape, or look up from a stand of reeds or the waters of the canal to see some other explorer staring down in disbelief? Will I be aware that anything is wrong or out of place?)

I plan to continue on into Area X, to go as far as I can before it is too late. I will follow my husband up the coast, up past the island, even. I don't believe I'll find him—I don't need to find him—but I want to see what he saw. I want to feel him close, as if he is in the room. And, if I'm honest, I can't shake the sense that he is *still here*, somewhere, even if utterly transformed—in the eye of a dolphin, in the touch of an uprising of moss, anywhere and everywhere. Perhaps I'll even find a boat abandoned on a deserted beach, if I'm lucky, and some sign of what happened next. I could be content with *just that*, even knowing what I know.

This part I will do alone, leaving you behind. Don't follow. I'm well beyond you now, and traveling very fast.

Has there always been someone like me to bury the bodies, to have regrets, to carry on after everyone else was dead?

I am the last casualty of both the eleventh and the twelfth expeditions.

I am not returning home.

ACKNOWLEDGMENTS

Thanks to my editor, Sean McDonald, for many kindnesses and for his wonderful edits to the novel. Thanks also to the great, dedicated crew at FSG who worked on the book—I really appreciate your efforts. Thanks to my agent, Sally Harding, and to all of the good people at the Cooke Agency. Much love to my wife, Ann, the only person with whom I can discuss works in progress, for her thoughts on the characters and situations. Thanks to my first readers—most of you know who you are—and in particular, Gregory Bossert, Tessa Kum, and Adam Mills for their extensive comments. Finally, thanks to the St. Marks National Wildlife Refuge: the people who work there and the people who care about it.

All three volumes of
Jeff VanderMeer's
Southern Reach trilogy
will be published in 2014

ANNIHILATION
February 2014

AUTHORITY
May 2014

ACCEPTANCE
September 2014